Into the Arms of

Madness

Other Books by Regina Pacelli

Outsmart the Unexpected: Grow Your Creativity the Edge-of-your-seat Way

Into the Arms of Madness

A Novel of Suspense

By

Regina Pacelli

ISBN-13: 978-1478122913

ISBN-10: 1478122919

Book cover design by Regina Pacelli. Royalty-free licensed photograph utilized in the cover design: PONTOON ON THE LAKE copyright © Aghizzi / Dreamstime.com

- 1 -

They say the morning after your wedding you wake up to a different person, someone who looks like the one you married, but who has begun to change in some subtle way. You can't put your finger on it, but you can feel the difference just the same.

I didn't quite believe that could be the case with my marriage. I had known my husband, Todd, for a year and a half before we got married. We were close and could talk for hours on every topic under the sun, and although we bickered on occasion, it was never about anything major. He was a good person – smart, easy-going, caring, funny, and loyal. I could always count on him to have my back.

I still thought this the morning after our wedding, but something in the way he looked at me at times left me with an uneasy feeling. I chalked it up to my imagination and just being tired from our wedding celebration and all the preparations leading up to it.

Todd had wanted to have a small, quiet ceremony—just the two of us. But we ended up inviting over forty people to our wedding. That was more for my benefit though since it was Todd's second marriage, my first, and I hoped the last for us both.

At Todd's suggestion, we had both written our own vows. I did not know what he had written until he spoke them to me at our wedding. He spoke the words with such a forceful earnestness, such force of will that I could feel them encircling me and shutting out all other thoughts. He meant what he said and he wanted me to be completely sure of it. I was. We were now Mr. and Mrs. Todd McCrary.

I was glad for the opportunity to talk with his family. I had become acquainted with some of his friends, but not anyone in his family, except for his younger brother, Craig, whom we took out to dinner once when he came to town on some business. Much of his family lived quite a distance away and I was happy that most of those we had invited accepted our invitation. They all arrived the day of the wedding and left shortly after the reception.

Todd had never brought me home for holidays or other family gatherings. Whenever he did visit his family, which wasn't often, he went by himself. He always seemed to prefer spending time with my family. We always talked to each other about everything, but he'd always clam up whenever the topic of his family came up, and a veil of melancholy would descend upon him. I let it alone and never pressed him about it. I hadn't really gotten to know very many of his long time friends either except in a superficial way. Most of the time, whenever we got together with friends, it was with my friends.

At one point during the reception, from across the room, I could see Todd sitting with my co-workers, totally engrossed in conversation. I was glad that they were getting along so well. His older sister Claire was sitting with them, faded into the background, looking displeased about something. Todd seemed to be averting her gaze. I had tried to engage her in conversation earlier in the day, but failed. She didn't come across as shy though. An aloof negativity emanated from her and I couldn't help feeling as if I was being judged or sized up somehow.

The rest of his family was friendlier, but left me feeling ill at ease also. His parents' smiles seemed plastered on. They kept remarking, whenever I was alone with them, about my nervousness and wedding day jitters and how we don't see things clearly when we're nervous and how we let our imaginations get the best of us. I did not feel at all nervous ... or jittery. I am not a nervous person. At least I didn't used to be.

I was also much slimmer than Todd's first wife whom they fondly remembered was pleasingly plump. "You need to put on a few pounds, Bridget dear. We couldn't tell you apart from the carrots and peas!" my mother-in-law said. My in-laws were full of peculiar expressions.

I had to work hard not to show my bafflement, which wasn't easy since I was increasingly hounded as the day wore on by the thought—well, peculiar expressions go together with peculiar people. I felt bad for thinking that though since I really didn't know them, and resolved to do my best and not draw any premature conclusions.

I kept smiling and tried to be as friendly and polite as I could, drawing on the customer service skills I'd honed in the two years since graduating from college. In my job as a customer service analyst, I always strived to keep my cool and be as helpful as possible. Many times, I would go well beyond what my supervisors advised and expected of me when helping a frustrated or discouraged customer with a difficult issue. I take great pride in that and it is the part of my job that I enjoy the most.

I interact with all sorts of personalities on a daily basis, some of whom can be quite curt or thoughtless, or even downright aggressive. But

Todd's parents were not the myriad of strangers I interacted with on a daily basis. They were becoming my extended family. I was becoming their daughter-in-law. It made no sense to me why they would talk to me about all sorts of negative things on my wedding day. In a short while, the 'why' became all too clear to me.

Even his younger brother seemed different from when I had met him a year ago. I think my family sensed something amiss also, but they said nothing. I think they didn't want to spoil our day. There's a time and place for everything, my mother would say.

- 2 -

The morning after our wedding, we were so spent from the previous day's excitement that we ended up sleeping much later than we had planned. We had wanted to get an early start on the long drive ahead of us and there was much to do before leaving for our honeymoon. But, when we finally did open our eyes, the desire for an early start had lost much of its appeal and we just lay there, entwined with the covers and each other, half-heartedly trying to convince ourselves to get up. We toyed with the idea of forgetting the trip and just staying right where we were, but we finally managed to get up and get cracking.

We were going to spend the week at a beautiful cabin by the lake that Todd had learned about from a friend of his. The photos of it that Todd showed me were magnificent. It was an idyllic place to spend our honeymoon—peaceful, pristine, and secluded. The owners, Emily and Malcolm, kept it for their own occasional use and rented it out the rest of the time to vacationers like us.

They seemed to be a very pleasant couple and even though they had no children, there was something very nurturing and maternal about Emily. I got along well with her and we had a few really long conversations.

According to the instructions that Emily gave us, the cabin was about two hours from the city, so it would be about a two and half to three-hour drive if traffic wasn't too bad in the city. The roads near the cabin were not clearly marked and we don't own a GPS, but Emily thought a GPS wouldn't be very useful in that area anyway. She provided us with a detailed map showing various landmarks to go by once we left the main route and told us to feel free to call if we had questions or ran into any problems along the way.

After a quick breakfast, I started packing for both of us, while Todd finished some business he had to take care of for work. Todd worked as a consultant and was currently serving as the technical lead on a large-scale computer infrastructure implementation. It was a field he had worked in since graduating from college five years ago. His client wanted him to provide feedback on a draft design document before he left. He had already read it and just needed to reply to them with his comments. Todd didn't expect it to take more than a couple of hours at most. He was so conscientious and dependable. That was something else I loved about him.

And he was lucky that he really enjoyed his job. A family friend had pulled some strings and gotten me my current customer service job since I hadn't been able to find anything in my chosen field upon graduation. I still could not find anything acceptable, for one reason or another, in the two years since graduating.

I had eventually settled on anthropology as my major, but had gone through several majors prior to that. At first, I had wanted to be a veterinarian since I loved being around animals so much. The course work, however, proved to be way too boring. So I switched my major to history and then finally settled on anthropology with thoughts of getting a research job. I found the myriad of possible cultures, past and present, to delve into fascinating.

My family and friends say I'm being too picky. Maybe they're right, but I don't think so. Hopefully, I'll be able to make use of some of the skills I'm acquiring when I do find something. In the meantime, I work as a customer service rep during the day and continue my reading and postgraduate studies at night.

And that's how I met Todd. In the first year of my post-graduate studies, I had to attend various two-hour lectures, on different related topics, the first Monday of every month. The lectures were open to the public and anyone who had an interest could attend. They were given in a large hall and at one particular lecture, Todd happened to be sitting a few rows in front of me. He kept looking in my direction, and when the lecture was finished, he came over and struck up a conversation with me. We took a liking to each other right from the start.

———

Neither of us wanted to bring along much baggage even though we were travelling by car, so I tried to keep it down to the essentials. And anyway, we had to leave enough room in the car for the groceries we were going to bring with us—lots of steaks for Todd, lots of veggies for me.

I wanted to bring some groceries with us. Emily told me the nearest grocery, except for a tiny mom and pop store, was a about a thirty minute drive from the cabin and I wanted to make sure we had some of our must-have favorites.

There wasn't much room left over in the trunk and back seat of Todd's car after I got all of our bags and the coolers containing the provisions loaded since Todd already had stuff in the trunk—a shovel, work gloves, jack, spare tire, flashlight, flares, and other emergency items. In trying to make room for everything, I also came across a box containing a rope, and what looked to me like a large hunting knife—the type you'd use to gut an animal. That seemed somewhat odd to me because Todd didn't hunt—at least not since I'd known him.

There was also, what appeared to be a small, handheld dart gun and some darts, and some other stuff. I took the box along with its contents out of the trunk to make some room, but left the other items. I put the box temporarily out of the way and when Todd was done with what he had to complete for work, I mentioned it to him.

"Yeah," he said. "I put it in the trunk a few days ago. One of my co-workers goes hunting a lot and he lent us some of his equipment. It's kind of a remote area, so I asked him to lend us some small items that would fit in the car with all of our other stuff. I thought I had mentioned it to you. Sorry."

He paused for a moment, studying the sudden worried expression that ripped across my face. I knew it was secluded. I had liked the idea—just Todd, me, and Mother Nature. I knew it best to be prepared. But thinking about the hunting knife gave me visions of possibilities I did not want to entertain.

He continued, trying to reassure. "Nothing will happen. I'm sure of it. What are the odds? Let's not put ourselves into a negative frame of mind. I only wanted us to bring along some extra stuff, just in case."

"Wouldn't a gun be better to have ... just in case?"

"He only owns hunting rifles and neither of us has ever handled one before. Anyway, he wasn't going to lend it to us."

"Yea. That makes sense. I'm glad you thought of borrowing some of those other things from him though. Good thinking!" I smiled. "It's beautiful out today. Perfect weather for driving," I said, changing the topic. I was still bothered by the thought, but didn't want to make a big deal about it. Todd got the box and went out to the car to find some room for it in the trunk while I locked up.

Todd's neighbors came outside to wish us well. I guess they were my neighbors also now since we were going to be living at Todd's place, until we bought a home of our own, because his place had more room. He had been renting the house from his next-door neighbors, the Montelbans. We had spent most of our time over by me while we were dating, but now that we were married, this seemed the most practical option for the time being.

We both wanted to find something away from the city, in a quiet area, where the houses weren't so close together that you couldn't help but hear your neighbors' business and they yours. Somewhere with more room for the children we hoped to have, but still close enough to the city so that we'd still have a reasonable commute to work.

I worked in the city and luckily, most of Todd's assignments were usually in the city as well. He did have to travel sometimes for his job, but his trips were usually short day trips, or at most, lasted only one or two days. The travelling didn't seem to wear on him at all. Todd seemed to thrive on it, looking quite refreshed whenever he returned home.

As Mrs. Montelban, an older woman in her early sixties or thereabouts, walked over to me, she shooed some cats away that were prowling around the garbage pails.

"There are always so many cats hanging around here the past few years," Mrs. Montelban said, clapping her hands as she made menacing gestures towards the cats. All the cats, except a brazen few, ran towards the backyard. The others moved underneath the porch and remained crouched there, staring at her, impatiently waiting for a safe opportunity to resume their activities.

"You make such a beautiful couple," Mrs. Montelban continued. "I'm so very glad that Todd found such a sweet and lovely young woman. He never dated anyone for very long before he met you. The longest relationship he had was with Lilly, a very impolite and selfish girl who made Todd very sad. It lasted only a couple of months. You've made such a positive change in him. He's so much more upbeat and happy these days."

She didn't mention Todd's first wife. It seemed Todd had not told Mrs. Montelban about her. I guess he had his reasons for not doing so, but still, I wondered *why not* mention her if he didn't seem to mind telling about the other women he had been dating before me.

Todd was a very outgoing person and we talked about so many things with each other and shared so much of what happened in our lives, but he had pieces of himself that I don't think he ever spoke about with anyone, not even me. I knew very little about his first wife—just that she had left him, and Mrs. Montelban didn't even know of her existence. In time, it was my hope that he would feel comfortable enough to share with me those areas of his life that he now guarded so closely.

"And he's done the same for me," I replied. "He's a great guy. I'm crazy about him," and I added, jokingly, as Todd came over to where we were standing, "even though he's not a vegetarian!"

"Don't listen to Bridget, Mrs. Montelban. She'll be getting you to banish your world-class pot roast I love so much and have you replacing it with vegetable lasagna if she has her way with you. Two weeks ago, Bridget declared meat the enemy. Maybe we can lure her back over to the dark side. Eh, Mrs. Montelban?" Todd winked at her and then put his arm around my shoulder as he gave me a peck on the cheek.

"I love meat!" I countered. "I just don't think it's good for you based on all that I've been reading about it lately. Soooo ... meat's *not* my enemy. We're just not on speaking terms anymore until it shapes up and changes its ways."

We all had a good laugh and talked for a few more minutes until Todd cut off Mrs. Montelban just as she began telling us what promised to be a long story about their own upcoming vacation plans. "Well, we'd better be shoving off now. It's a long drive," Todd said, starting to move towards the car.

She continued telling us their vacation plans as she walked with us to the car. Todd really liked her, but got annoyed with her sometimes because she had a knack for starting long conversations when he was in a hurry.

Mr. Montelban, who hadn't said much until now, chimed in and wished us a safe trip. He suggested that we get together for dinner after Todd and I returned home from our honeymoon and were all settled in. Mrs. Montelban gave us both a big hug and kiss. Mr. Montelban, more reserved than she, just smiled and said, "Don't worry about anything here. We'll keep an eye on things for you."

As I hugged Mrs. Montelban, I glanced over her shoulder and saw that one of the cats had ventured out from underneath the front porch and was busy trying to remove the lid off one of the nearby vinyl garbage pails.

- 3 -

Once we left the city and turned onto Route 66, there was about an hour stretch where we didn't have to stay so focused on looking out for various signs and turn-offs. I was driving and we planned to switch places and find somewhere to eat lunch and stretch our legs a bit, after we turned off Route 66.

I was listening to the upbeat music we had been playing since we left, while Todd was reading a book—well sort of reading. Whenever I took my eyes off the road to glance over at him, he appeared to be lost in thought; looking at the book that he had open on his lap, but not really seeing the words. Every once in a while he'd turn a page.

He had been in a very energetic and positive frame of mind when we left and we had been having a good time singing along, in our not even close to American Idol voices, to some oldies tunes. We always loved to do that, especially on long drives. But midway through one of the songs, he said he didn't really feel like singing anymore and that he was just going to read for a bit. He fell into a deep state of contemplation and didn't appear to notice when I turned off the music.

Todd was like that for quite some time. I was about to say something to try to lighten his mood and bring him back to me from the far off place he'd gone to, but before I could, he asked me somewhat tentatively, "You know I love you, right?"

We always teased each other and often good-naturedly bantered back and forth. He could say things, joking around, with a deadly serious expression on his face. My instincts had let me down on many an occasion and as such I couldn't rely too heavily on them, so I teased him back even though in my gut I sensed that this particular time he wasn't teasing me.

"Perhaps ... but probably not as much as you love Mrs. Montelban and her roast beef, I imagine!" I grinned at him expecting him to come back at me with some hysterically witty reply that would leave me in stitches. He just looked at me, his eyes intent on me answering his question. He added, "For better or worse, right?"

He was serious. I didn't know what had gotten into him, but whatever it was, it had now travelled across the front seat of the car and grabbed hold of me as well.

I said, "You're the best person I know. I would do anything for you. And, yes, for better or worse. And, yes, I love you." I thought, nothing like having a serious conversation while you're driving on the highway. "I don't usually go around marrying people I don't love. Why?"

"Well, there's love and then there's *love*."

"And then there's popcorn. C'mon. Quit the riddles. Tell me! It can't be that bad. Is it that bad?"

"I don't really want to talk about it now. Not in the car. We'll have plenty of time later to talk about it."

I just gave him a quick look of 'this *better not be* your idea of a ha ha ha so hysterical practical joke' – my brow suitability knitted for emphasis. I enticed him to come closer, emanating thoughts of ... honeymoon = romance ... i.e. no practical jokes, funny man.

Todd had a penchant for suspense and for playing practical jokes. The thought came to me that maybe he wasn't planning a practical joke. Maybe he was planning a wonderful, romantic surprise. That would be nice.

By this time, we had just about reached the Route 66 exit that we needed to take. From here on in, we would be travelling on smaller roads and eventually on the back road that led to the cabin. We travelled awhile more, keeping an eye out for somewhere to grab a bite to eat and casually surveying the towns we passed through for any interesting places we might want to come back to during the week.

We passed a number of restaurants and shops, each one a reflection of the owner's personality and circumstances. Some establishments were thriving, alive and vibrant, casting an overarching shadow that relegated their neighbors into the margins of the merchant community.

These marginalized stores, of unfortunate merchants that had fallen on hard times, increased in number the further away from Route 66 we travelled. The owners beckoned the passersby with extra large smiles or deep discounts and entertainment that were not to be missed, seemingly reaching out with soulful eyes and cup in hand, begging potential customers to please overlook the bit of peeling paint here or a boarded up window there because there was no extra money to get it fixed.

On one particular stretch of road, many of the homes were badly in need of repair and almost every block had a for sale sign on at least one house. The surrounding area was beautiful, with heavily tree-lined streets and property lots that seemed very well thought out. At one point in its past, I imagined that it must have been a growing and happy community. It piqued my curiosity and I made a mental note to ask Emily about it when I spoke with her again.

Todd dropped me off in front of a busy cafe so that I could order lunch for us while he drove over to a nearby gas station to fuel up the car. We both felt a little bit guilty stopping at one of the places that were doing well instead of one that was more in need of our patronage, but we figured that the food would be fresher and didn't want to chance it at one of the other establishments. Last thing we'd need is digestive troubles on our honeymoon.

By the time Todd got back to the cafe, lunch had come and his order of rare steak and fried potatoes was already starting to get cold. We thought it was only going to take a few minutes to gas up the car, but he had been gone a good twenty minutes.

I saw him standing by the door and waved to him. This caught the attention of at least one of the diners. I noticed her out of the corner of my eye. She followed my gaze over to Todd, then snapped her head back and tried to blend herself into the background, putting her hat back on and pulling it down as far onto her head she could, obscuring much of her face. An odd reaction, I thought.

I looked more closely at her for a few moments. She was sitting in a booth with two other people, a man and a woman. They were both talking and laughing about something. She was not. She was looking down at the bowl of soup in front of her, slowly stirring it with a spoon. She stole a quick glance at me and became distressed when she caught me now staring in her direction. She hurriedly looked away from me, retreating into herself, and resumed stirring her soup. She looked so fragile. I didn't know what her trouble was, but I felt sorry for her.

Todd had returned my wave, but didn't immediately start walking over to our table. He stood where he was, erect and sure, surveying the room for a minute. He had a commanding presence and his tall stature and deep-set eyes added to that effect. It was an effect could also be unintentionally intimidating to people who did not know him very well.

The cafe was packed and the waitress had already given me the check when she brought over our food. She had asked when I was ordering whether we might want any coffee or dessert afterwards or anything else. I had told her no, and since it was so busy, I asked her if she could give me the check now, which she did.

Todd plopped himself down in the seat opposite me and began relating what had transpired on his quest to fill up the gas tank, his mood considerably brighter than before. I listened and as I did, I watched him pour half a bottle of steak sauce (*ok, that's an exaggeration, but not by much*) over both the steak and the potatoes and then start inhaling his meal. I had starting eating before he got to the cafe, but even with that head start, I was still just halfway done by the time he finished downing his last bit of potato.

"Sorry it took so long. There was only one attendant at the station and they didn't have any self-service pumps so I had to wait while the attendant took care of the two cars that were ahead of me," Todd said. "And he was really taking his time with them. The attendant—I think he said his name was Dan—asked me where I was I heading. I didn't want to be rude, but it isn't really anyone's business. He's a complete stranger. I wasn't going to tell him 'we're on our honeymoon and heading up to a cabin on Pawtucket Lake'. So, I told him that we were on our way to Ulster. He seemed satisfied with that."

"Ulster? Where's that?"

"It's a few towns past where we're staying. To the northeast, I think. The name stuck in my head when I was looking at a map of the area. I'm glad he didn't start questioning me further, and asking me where we'd be staying in Ulster. Anyway, Dan started telling me about the trouble he's been having with his wife lately."

"Yes. I know. She's become a vegetarian."

"Noooo," he said, grinning, his eyes smiling. "He wouldn't still have such an air of sanity about him if that were the case."

"Ha. Ha … So what's the trouble then?" I said. My curiosity was piqued.

"From what he told me, she loves nature and being outdoors and frequently goes bird watching in the woods. She even wrote two books about birds. But she's hardly been outside in the past few weeks and then when she does go out, it's not for very long.

"She was studying some birds a few weeks ago and a group of people came up on her suddenly and kind of closed in on her and began talking to her, not attacking her physically, but she felt threatened and it made her very upset.

"Not you though, Bre. You're not so easily rattled. Sweet, but deadly!" he joshed, reaching his hand across the table to mooch another one of my fries. I didn't know about that though. I was good in emergency situations. Any situation, really, that required you to keep a cool head. But, being outnumbered when you're alone in the woods, away from the earshot of anyone who could assist or serve as a deterrent, I wasn't sure what I'd do. I hoped never to find out.

"Maybe I'd just faint from fright."

His smile vanished. "Always keep your eyes peeled when you're alone and if a situation doesn't feel right to you, get away from it as fast as you can. She probably wasn't paying attention to her surroundings. That's how they were able to sneak up on her. Don't take any foolish chances," he said trying to press his words deep into my unconscious. He waited for me to acknowledge him.

"Eyes peeled. Yes, sir!" I saluted him.

"I don't want to see you taking any foolish chances."

"When have you ever seen me taking foolish chances?"

"Well. Just don't contemplate taking any in the future. I want to keep you around a while longer ...

At least until after the honeymoon." Todd winked at me.

"Oh, brother!" I said, rolling my eyes.

He continued with his story. "Dan managed to get his wife to go out today though. She went out to lunch with their neighbors ... actually, she's having lunch at this cafe. This place is pretty popular it seems."

I thought about the woman I had seen earlier. "Maybe that's her in the booth by the window behind you."

Todd craned his neck around to have a look. "Possibly. It could be any one of the women here. He didn't describe her at all. Anyway, that's what took me so long. Oh, hey," Todd said, remembering. "Dan mentioned a great place we can go for dinner. They even have live music. Maybe we can give it a try one night this week."

"Sure," I replied, only half paying attention. My mind was still fixated on the story Todd had just related to me. "I think that's her. She seems pretty upset about something." Todd had lost interest in it though.

"I can feel my stress dissolving already," he said. "It'll be great to relax by the lake. I'm glad we decided to honeymoon here rather than someplace we'd end up having to be more on the go."

I pushed my plate over to him. "I am totally stuffed. This omelet's huge … I can't eat another bite." Todd dug his fork in, and two large mouthfuls later, all traces of my omelet were gone.

- 4 -

By the time we reached the cabin, it was already late in the afternoon. The winding, narrow dirt road leading up to it took us to the cabin's back door. The front of the cabin faced the lake, which was directly beyond the deck attached to the front of the house. The surrounding property was large, the mailbox being a good quarter of a mile away at the beginning of the dirt road. We didn't see any homes as we approached the turn-off to the cabin. We did see other similar narrow dirt roads interspersed along the way, but they offered no more of a clue as to what lay at the end than the road we had just travelled on.

We wanted to relax and perhaps explore a bit of the property, but first on the agenda was getting the car unpacked and putting away the groceries we had brought with us.

The key was exactly where Emily said it would be, in a small metal container hooked underneath the overhang of the front deck. There were two keys. One that would unlock both the front and back doors, the other for a large shed near the dock.

We stood there for a while, taking in our surroundings, before going into the house. One of the first things I noticed was the air. It smelled so wonderful and fresh. You couldn't help feeling energized and renewed by it. I wished I could bottle it and take it home with me, maybe take a whiff before a difficult exam to bolster me up.

The lake had a very uneven shape to it and we couldn't easily judge exactly how large it was, although from what we could see of it, it appeared to be quite expansive. Some homes were visible on the far side of the lake and from our vantage point I could see a smaller home, where the lake curved, on our side. The homes across the lake were much larger than Emily and Malcolm's and were snuggly nestled between tall stands of trees.

No one seemed to be doing any boating on the lake, but perhaps it was too late in the day for it. We didn't even see anyone out and about at the water's edge.

I had seen how beautiful the lake and the outside of the cabin were in the photos Todd had shown me, but the cabin looked a lot larger in person and paled in comparison to the interior. Befitting its location, it had a rustic motif, and everything from the woodwork to the furniture to even the layout and appliances in the kitchen was top-of-the-line.

There was a full complement of pots, utensils, and dishes in the kitchen and Emily had even made sure that the refrigerator and pantry were fully stocked. She hadn't told us about that beforehand. A handwritten note welcoming us, on charmingly designed stationary, was taped to the front of the refrigerator door.

I appreciated their thoughtfulness, but wished they'd have told us about the food. There was hardly any room in the refrigerator for the perishables we had brought along and as I was pondering whether to take some of the less perishable items out of the fridge, Todd rumbled through the back door with the last of our stuff.

He started opening and closing the cabinets, searching for something. "I moved the car where it will stay out of the sun. There's a nice spot a little further from the cabin, in the shade."

He smiled, having found the glass he was after, and filled it with some water from the tap. "I brought the rest of the bags upstairs. You're gonna love the master bedroom, Bre. It has a sitting area with a fabulous view of the lake and all around the room there are vases filled with fresh cut flowers … Almost done putting the groceries away? Let's take our walk around the rest of the property before it gets too late for it."

I was puzzled. Fresh cut flowers? Emily and Malcolm must have been here earlier or else, I guess, had someone come and set things up for us. Todd didn't seem surprised or fazed at all by it.

I handed him the welcome note and told him, "I'm trying to see what I can take out of the fridge. It's packed. I think Emily mentioned that there's another refrigerator in the basement."

Todd's eyes narrowed and his lips clamped down around his clenched teeth. He had a tendency to do that whenever he was bothered by something that he considered an avoidable annoyance.

"I can bring some stuff down there," I suggested and began the process of reorganizing some of the refrigerator's contents.

"No. You finish things here. Give them to me. I'll bring them downstairs for you."

"Hey, look at this Todd. She's got a bottle of your favorite wine in here. The little devil! She started talking about wine when I last spoke with her and somewhere in the middle of our conversation I mentioned what wine you like and that I'm not really partial to wine and seldom drink alcohol."

As I continued to search the rest of the refrigerator and freezer, it became more and more apparent to me that they really wanted to make us feel taken care of. I started wondering why they even *wanted* to rent out the cabin in the first place. They certainly didn't seem to need the income it would bring.

Finally, everything in the kitchen was put away and we were free to go and look around outside.

"Maybe we can find one of our neighbors and get acquainted, let them know we're staying here. We're only going to be here a short while, I know, but it would be nice to know where some of our neighbors are," I said.

We had looked forward to spending the week by ourselves, so I quickly added, "Just in case we have an emergency, not to spend any time with them necessarily." He walked over to the back door and bent down to pick up my brown leather sandals.

"I guess we can take the path back out to the main road and walk up one of the turn-offs we passed," he said, as he began walking over to me. "It might be easier than trying to find them by walking along the water's edge ... Actually it might be even easier if we take one of the boats out tomorrow. We'd have a better view of any nearby homes from the lake. We can take the boat up to their dock and go see if anyone's home."

"Alright, we'll do it tomorrow," I replied, looking at the sandals Todd was dangling in front of me. He stood there waiting for me to take them and put them on.

Since my teenage years, I have never worn shoes in the house, or slippers for that matter, in the spring or summer time—not if I could help it. The first thing I did whenever I came home was to fling off my shoes and let my feet out of their little prison cells. I always walked around barefoot inside and sometimes I did outside as well if I was going to sit on a deck or patio or relax on the grass.

"I don't know how you can walk around without shoes." Todd extended the sandals further in my direction.

I took the sandals from him and slid them onto my feet. Grinning at him, I said, "My feet like their freedom."

"Well, they're not going to like it so much when you end up stepping on a shard of wood or glass or something falls on your foot. What am I going to do with you?" He smiled and kissed me, and his good-natured scolding took on a softer tone. "I don't want you going down the basement or walking around outside in your bare feet."

"I won't. I promise," I said, placating him, but having no intention of complying (or catering really) to his silly worrying.

Todd wanted to make a quick call on his cell phone to a work associate of his, which turned into a not so quick call. We started on our walk as he was making his call and I led the way. He followed alongside, not really paying attention to which way we were heading. The phone conversation was absorbing most of his attention, so much so that he almost fell after tripping over a tree root.

He made the call because he wanted to make sure that his co-worker had gotten and understood the information that he had e-mailed earlier in the day. In his e-mail, he had asked her to give him a call so that he could go over certain things that would be easier to discuss over the phone. He discussed them with her for a while and after inquiring whether she had everything she needed—and she did—he said goodbye and told her to call if she ran into any problems.

"Glad that's off my mind. I don't like anything outstanding hanging over my head," he said, putting his phone back in the phone case on his belt.

"She's not going to keep calling with questions, is she?"

"No. I doubt it. I've worked on a few projects with her and she never does. She didn't call me even though I had asked her to. *I* had to call *her*. I was just trying to be polite. That's all."

I took us in a big circle around the cabin, not wanting to stray too far away, but our ambitions proved to be greater than our energy and we headed back to the house before too long. In less than an hour after we had started our walk, we were relaxing in a couple of lounge chairs down by the lake and ended up falling asleep.

It was already early evening by the time we awoke. Todd woke up before me, and when I finally opened my eyes, his head was facing in my direction. He was staring at me. His lips instantly turned into a smile—a rather mischievous smile. He stood up and offered me his hand, keeping hold of mine as we walked the short distance back to the cabin.

"I'll cook dinner for us tonight," Todd blurted out, just as we were reaching the door. His voice had a very emphatic I-will-brook-no-dissent tone to it. Todd was never very fond of cooking, so this sudden desire caught me off-guard. Whenever we ate together at home, I always did the cooking, so I didn't know what had brought on this unexpected culinary urge.

"Why don't you relax and take a nice soothing bath while I get dinner ready," he continued. "You didn't see the upstairs yet. The bathroom's spectacular!"

"No. I haven't yet seen it," I said, grinning. "Somebody—I don't remember who—was hurrying me to finish up in the kitchen so we could go for a walk."

"Go ahead. I'll call you when dinner's ready."

"It's okay. I'll cook."

"No. I insist. Besides, I have a special surprise for you."

"What kind of surprise?" I asked.

"You'll have to wait and see, but I think you'll be pleased." Todd winked at me and opened the door. "We'll have a nice dinner and then we can relax over some coffee in the living room and continue the discussion we began in the car."

My head was starting to ache, so having a soak in the tub did sound rather nice. I was married to a man that loved suspense, so I resolved to go with the flow of that—or try to at least.

The master bedroom and bath were just as Todd described. I started unpacking some of our stuff, but then curiosity got the better of me. Positioning myself at the top of the stairs, I listened for Todd's movements, trying to see if I could tell a little bit about the surprise. My resolve hadn't lasted very long. He was making very little noise though. That was so annoying. I toyed with the idea of going down the stairs, or at least part of the way down, to gain a better listening and peeking vantage point, but then decided that I wasn't really curious enough to potentially ruin his surprise by getting caught peeking. I would wait to know what it was.

The thought of a soak in the tub had sounded nice when Todd first mentioned it, but I ended up not taking one.

Instead, I just washed up a bit, changed into a sleeveless shift dress that Todd had always found attractive, and sat in the armchair by the window in the master bedroom, waiting, alternately dozing and quietly meditating (*or at least attempting to*), and looking out upon the eerie beauty of the lake. The shadows that the setting sun cast upon the lake in the evening created an entirely different atmosphere from in the daytime; serenity was replaced by a mysterious beauty.

- 5 -

After a long while, I felt a gentle hand on my shoulder. It didn't startle me at all. I had become that relaxed.

"Everything's ready."

I turned my head to look up at Todd. He was wearing a perfectly pressed black shirt and pants, black shoes, and had slicked back his hair. I didn't remember packing those clothes. Todd saw my questioning expression and interrupted it with, "Come, sweetheart. Everything's ready. Let's go downstairs."

Something in me made me hold my tongue. I couldn't respond. I just took the hand that Todd offered me and got up out of the chair, and as I did, I could see a tray on the table near the door with two long stem glasses on it filled with a red colored liquid that I assumed was wine. Todd walked over to the table and picked up the glasses and handed one of them to me, then raised his glass.

"To our future together. May we never be parted. May our love never fade." Todd tapped his glass against mine and took a sip, paused to look at me, then drank the rest.

I took a sip from my glass as well, and then stopped. It was indeed wine. Todd knew I never drank the stuff. He kissed me and whispered, "Drink all of it, Bre. For us. To bring us a long and happy future together."

Doing my best not to wince at the taste of it, I drank it all down and smiled as I handed him back the emptied glass, not wanting to start his surprise off on the wrong foot. I was beginning to think that he had a wonderful romantic surprise planned after all and not one of his practical jokes. But I was still a bit troubled by the thought of the upcoming after dinner conversation he had mentioned earlier.

From the top of the stairs, I could see that the lights were turned down low. The warm glow of candlelight was flickering against the wall. In silence, we descended the stairs and Todd slowly led me into the dining room. He had transformed the rustic charm of the room into something quite romantic. I was speechless, but Todd could see that I was pleased and a bit awed by the whole thing. He proceeded to lead me over to the table, pulled out my chair for me, and with a flourish of his hand motioned for me to sit down. He had never pulled my chair out for me before, not even on our first date. Todd was going for the full effect.

After handing me a single red rose, taken from the crystal vase adorning the center of the table, he disappeared into the kitchen. Its entryway was closed off by a sliding door so that any light from the kitchen would be blocked and not diminish the romantic ambiance created by the candlelight.

I sat there waiting, my relaxed state evolving into a dreamy mellowness—an effect of the wine no doubt and the soft mesmerizing effect of the vanilla and sandalwood scented candles. Before too long Todd re-emerged from the kitchen, pushing a serving cart over to the table. There were two large dishes on the cart, kept warm by stainless steel plate covers. Next to them was a pitcher of water, an ice bucket, and a bowl of red grapes.

Todd placed the items on the white vinyl lace tablecloth that was a little bit too big for the table and sat in the chair opposite me, across the short side of the table. Our plates were still covered. He reached both hands across the table seeking mine and I grabbed hold of them. He said nothing. He just looked into my eyes for a few moments, squeezed my hands, heightening the sense of drama, smiled lovingly, and then quietly said, "Let's eat," as he let go of my hands. Todd uncovered his plate. It was a large rare steak with potatoes and peas. No surprise there. I wondered what was on my plate. I sat there, passively, without opening the cover. My dreamy mellowness was fading.

"Go ahead. You'll be pleased," he assured me, as he cut his steak and took a large mouthful.

I took the cover off and stared down in disbelief at my plate. I couldn't believe it. I looked at Todd who was eagerly anticipating a positive reaction from me. So, no romance. Practical joke after all, it seemed.

My plate also had potatoes and peas on it. It also had a small steak, although mine was at least well-done. I didn't pick up my knife or fork. I just sat there trying to figure out what to say. I didn't know what to say.

"I had Emily get it especially for you. It's the very best grass-fed organic beef you can find. I know you've become concerned about the current state of meat and that's why you've sworn off eating it, but this meat has none of the issues you're so worried about. It's delicious and very healthy for you. I thought it would be a nice surprise. Don't worry about the cost. Emily knows of some places where we can get it at quite a sizable discount. So, now you won't have to feel like you have to forgo eating meat anymore."

Hearing what he had to say began dissolving any negative feelings that the surprise had provoked, slowly replacing them with a sense of comfort and appreciation that he had gone to all this trouble. But,

I still couldn't figure out why he wanted to make it a surprise in the first place. Another thing that bothered me was that he seemed to be having all these conversations and arrangements that I was unaware of. I wondered if he had been the one to ask Emily to place all the fresh cut flowers throughout the cabin.

I don't really have a suspicious nature and I didn't know what had gotten into me. I was probably making too much out of it. He was just being thoughtful and he was fond of surprising people. It was nothing more than that. I was so caught up in my thoughts, chastising myself for thinking even slightly ill of Todd's actions, that I had left him hanging, waiting for a response. I couldn't even imagine how much distress the expressions on my face, through all these thoughts, had caused him.

"Tell me you're pleased, Bre." My silence was starting to erode the romantic ambiance that had filled the room just a few short minutes before.

He did it for me, although I think he did it a little bit for himself as well, wanting my diet back the way it used to be, at least to some degree.

I smiled. "Thank you. I *am* pleased. Really I am. It's just that I was taken by surprise. I didn't know what to say. That's all."

"I want to see you eat the whole thing," he happily urged me on.

"That won't be a problem. I'm feeling kind of hungry tonight. Anyway, I know if I can't finish it all, it won't go to waste. You'll help me out."

"Nah. This steak is all yours, my love."

I beamed at him as I dug into my steak. It was good, really good. I was sorry I had taken the oomph out of his surprise and determined to show my appreciation for his thoughtfulness. "It's fabulously delicious."

I wanted to ask him about the flowers, just to get it off my mind, but I couldn't bring myself to.

We remained at the table for a long time after we finished eating, discussing our plans for the next day and happily musing about the future. We were starting to feel married.

Getting up from the table, Todd suggested that I head into the living room area to relax for a few minutes while he brought us the coffee. When I offered to help or at least help with clearing the table, he said that he'd take care of it. "Go ahead into the living room. Coffee's already made. Just need to warm it up a bit. I'll bring it in. Won't take but a minute or two." He then proceeded to put the dishes onto the serving cart and disappeared into the kitchen.

The minute or two drew out into ten minutes. I had done enough damage to his surprise without meaning to already so I didn't call out to him. However long it took him, I was going to sit and wait. Fifteen minutes passed. Then twenty minutes turned into twenty-five. Finally, after thirty minutes, Todd came into the living room, without the coffee, and sat down next to me on the sofa.

He looked serious and anxious, but said nothing. He only moved closer to me so that his arm was pressed up against mine. My hands were resting in my lap and Todd took hold of one of them, and tightly pressed it between both of his. I placed my other hand on top of his trembling hands.

Before I could say anything to him, a silent parade of people walked into the living room startling me, and shattering the last vestiges of peacefulness that I had been feeling while waiting for Todd to return. They were all just as serious as Todd, and seemed confident and resolute. Todd's mother walked in first, followed by his father, and then three others, a woman and two men, that I didn't recognize.

Speaking softly into my ear, Todd said, "My parents you know and right behind them are Emily and my Uncle Malcolm, dad's older brother. The other gentleman is a—"

Todd stopped, sensing my apprehensiveness, and squeezed my hand tighter, but it did little to slow my heart, which was now pounding against my rib cage and in my ears.

"Trust me, Bre. Everything will be okay. I love you."

Resisting the impulse to yell my response, I replied, in a barely audible voice, with questions I was afraid to know the answer to. "*What* will be ok? What is this all about, Todd. Tell me. Please, tell me."

I think I was too scared to speak loud enough for anyone except Todd to hear. My tongue felt so thick, I barely got the words out, and my stomach was churning and beginning to make me feel queasy. I thought 'please, I can't throw up. Not now. Calm down. I have to calm down'.

"Shhh ... Shhh," he gently whispered and discretely motioned to me to remain still and not speak.

They all seated themselves, except for that one unidentified man who remained standing behind Emily and Malcolm. Emily sat there without looking at me, only looking down into her lap. The Emily I knew, the helpful, maternal woman that I so happily and pleasantly chatted with on the phone, as

I made the arrangements for our honeymoon stay here at her cabin, had all but disappeared. Hope was not to be had from her husband Malcolm either. He sat there just as passively as his wife did.

The tall man with deep-set eyes and scarred hands standing behind them was an impenetrable wall. His rigid stance and the stern, stone-cold expression on his face made me quickly turn my head towards Todd, in hopes he'd be able to offer some reassurance. But Todd was intently staring at his mother and father who nodded their heads slightly as if giving their assent for something.

His mother's very subdued expression was one of care and love for her son. This was so different from when I'd seen her last, on our wedding day, but she did not extend that warm feeling in my direction. I felt disconnected from her and the others, with no positive vibes or acknowledgement of any kind being directed my way.

With the cue received from his parents, Todd, still holding my hand, moved his lower body so that he could face me more directly. He locked onto my eyes, and the sense of love and care I saw in his helped the pounding of my heart subside to a dull roar.

He began talking to me.

"I don't know how to explain everything to you so that you'll understand. I want so much for you to understand. I'm hoping with your background, your interest in and fascination with different cultures, and the love I know you feel for me, that it will be easier for you than for most others.

"In the past, people outside of our culture always looked upon us with fear and revulsion and most could not understand or accept our beliefs and practices. Some that did initially accept us, or tried to, eventually turned their backs on us and ended up betraying us. We never felt safe. We were always put in the position of having to defend our ideas and even our very lives. At one sad point in our history, the tide turned against us so strongly that we were brutally and mercilessly hunted down and slaughtered by people who misinterpreted our traditions, and therefore hated us.

"So, it was decided that we would blend more fully into the mainstream of society and not be so open about our beliefs.   This choice let our community, which was on the verge of being extinguished about four or five generations ago, to begin growing again, albeit slowly and carefully.

"With a few exceptions, it is only through marriage that we let others into our world today. Because of our still diminished numbers, it seemed this was the best course of action to rebuild ourselves with the least risk to our community. We have resolved that each of us will marry someone carefully selected from outside of our community. Then as part of the post-marriage ritual, the tentative process of revealing our world to our mates and acquainting them with it begins—under the watchful eye of the other community members, of course, since we've seen that love can sometimes make a person behave rather unwisely.

"Emily was brought into the community by Malcolm and they have been happily married for over twenty years.   Sadly, Emily let us know that she was not able to bear any children and apologized for telling Malcolm otherwise before they married. She would not tell us why she could not bear children, but the reasons were so painful to her that she would not allow any doctors to examine her further. Normally, this would be an issue since each family is obligated to have at least two children, but since it took Malcolm three tries to find a wife who could truly embrace our customs, and since the community quickly became very fond of her, it was excused. Emily has contributed greatly in other ways though. Her maternal nature has eased the transition for quite a few new community members. She will help you too, as we all will try to.

"Ours is a great culture, Bre. Our beliefs and rituals give us strength. They vitalize us and bind us together. We strongly believe—no, we know—that it is because of them that each of us has been able to achieve success in our own personal endeavors. Some have achieved more success than others have, but none of us has ever experienced any degree of financial hardship. We have never wanted for anything, except acceptance, and perhaps, at times, love.

"I've told you that some individuals we took into our confidence failed us. I'm sorry to say that my first wife was one of them. She said she understood, but I came to realize after a few days that it was a lie, a lie she eventually admitted to my face. She couldn't truly understand us and the growing look of revulsion on her face as I began to school her in our ways was too much for me to take. She broke my heart. Please don't fail me, Bre. I don't want to live my life alone. I want a wife. I want to build a family of my own. And I want to do it with you."

I managed to stutter an, "I won't fail you. I promise." I had never stuttered before in my life. I prayed that no one, and especially not Todd, would interpret it in any negative way. I tried to smile in an attempt to deflect his attention from it, but the most I could muster was a weak, timid half turn of my lips.

I braced myself for the further explanations to come and kept my eyes focused on Todd, afraid of what I might see if I looked around the room at the others and even more so, worried about how I might react to what I saw. I couldn't even bring myself to look at Emily. I just told myself to keep taking slow, deep breaths. I reassured myself that they were probably a bit eccentric, that their practices and beliefs would most likely be nothing that I couldn't handle or—as Todd put it—understand.

I fought against the undigested food in my churning stomach that was threatening to push its way out of my stomach and up into my throat. I couldn't understand why Todd would want to have this type of discussion directly after dinner. Was it on purpose? Was it a test of what anxiety his revelations would provoke in me? I throw up my meal. I fail. Goodness. This promised to be a long night and already I did not understand what I was hearing.

I wanted the Todd I knew back—the Todd from this morning and all our yesterdays. Hopes for a beautiful honeymoon, a beautiful life together, were receding and being overshadowed by confusion, trepidation, and sadness. Oddly, I wasn't upset with Todd for not telling me any of this before we married. I knew I probably should have been upset, but I loved him and was starting to realize that this was probably what had been troubling him all along and making him sullen and remote on occasion. I tried my best to stay positive, to keep an open mind, and to suppress the fearful fantasies and premature conclusions swirling about my head. I believed Todd to be a good person. Things would work out.

He pressed on, seemingly accepting my reply.

"What I am about to tell you and everything the community will teach you about our practices and beliefs, you must never tell anyone in any way. And I mean *anyone*. Not your family. Not your friends. No one. I need your solemn vow that you will never reveal even the minutest detail to another living soul and that you will always be conscious of and guard against inadvertently bringing any outside attention to our community.

"The others have urged me to make you aware that any past members of our community that we had reason to suspect were even contemplating violating their promise, regretted it. Our community is not forgiving of those who seek to put us in harm's way. This may seem harsh, but in order to ensure our survival, it is unfortunately a necessary law that we must all live by.

"I hope we have your promise. Do we, Bre?"

I hesitated, my overloaded brain trying hard to process the new information he had just dumped on me. It was exhausting.

Todd asked again a few seconds later. This time more emphatically, the strong, direct tone of his voice pressing me into responding.

In a knee-jerk way, I replied, "Yes," without knowing what I was agreeing to. Almost as soon as I'd said yes, I wished I'd have said that I could not promise anything without first knowing more. But it did not seem likely that he would say any more without my promise and not promising would possibly create an impassable gulf between Todd and me. A favorite saying of a girlfriend of mine flashed through my mind: 'The only way out is through.' She whole-heartedly endeavored to live her life by this simple philosophy, but in my experience, all twenty-four years of it, I found that this approach to dealing with problems could bring its own kind of troubles and that sometimes, the best course of action is to take a step back, or sideways, or find a way around.

My mind was bouncing all over the place. A horrible thought seized me, that this may well be an elaborate, very un-funny setup from my practical joke loving husband. If it was or if this was some bonding ritual that his twisted imagination came up with, he would never live it down and I would absolutely, without a doubt figure out a way to give him a dose of his own medicine and cure him of it once and for all. Somehow, though, thinking it might be a practical joke calmed me. I actually preferred that explanation to the alternative explanations my imagination was assaulting me with. But, boy, if it was, he managed to enlist quite a few accomplices. If it was a joke, shame on his parents for participating.

I stole a quick peek out of the corner of my eye at his parents. They were sitting there, serious faced and completely still.

Feeling a bit bolder, I thought 'you're busted! Very well executed joke though, my evil genius. Twisted and sick, but very well executed. Now cut it out and let's get on with our honeymoon.'

I moved over on the sofa, several inches away from Todd, loosened my hand from his, and looked down into my lap. I said, as quietly and gently as I could, "You're not just pulling my leg with all this, are you?" It was the least offensive way I could think to ask the question, just in case my hopeful guess proved wrong.

With my head still lowered, I quickly scanned the faces around the room. They all appeared somewhat disappointed, except for Emily, who now looked worried. Genuinely worried. I focused my eyes on the floor and said nothing further. I waited for Todd to respond, but only a stifling silence filled the air. After an eternity—twenty seconds or so— Todd tenderly grasped my hand and I was able to exhale. It seemed that my questioning of his sincerity hadn't done any irreparable damage and I was grateful for that.

"Look at me, Bre."

I was afraid to, afraid I'd see the same look of disappointment on his face that I had seen on the faces of the others or worse.

With his other hand, Todd gently placed his fingers under my chin, turned my head towards his, and then pushed away a strand of hair that had fallen across my face and my still downcast eyes.

"It's alright," he said. "I know it's a bit much to take in. I'm not pulling your leg. This is not something I would joke about. Truly, it's not. Our rituals are hard, even for me.

"Poor, Bre. What a honeymoon you're having. Sorry it feels like it's spoiled for you, but it will get better. We'll have a wonderful life together. My parents are skeptical, but I'm not. I know you love me. I know you will understand and accept us. Accept me. I just have a few key things left to tell you at this point after which you can ask us any lingering questions you may have. Okay?"

I nodded my assent and looked up into his eyes. This made Todd smile. He was happy.

Relieved, Todd continued, "I told you that it is from our practices—our rituals—that we derive our success in life. One of our practices is that we hunt. We hunt, capture, and ultimately kill and eat our prey—prey that has qualities, strongly embedded, that would benefit and sustain us and make us stronger or smarter or healthier, prey that has whatever qualities our community needs. During a transference ceremony, those sought after qualities become part of us.

"The person who became the steak you ate tonight was selected especially for you by Emily and Malcolm. He was a health conscious distance runner and his blood was blended into the wine you drank earlier. You must feel his strength taking hold in your blood. You didn't throw up before even though you felt frightened. It was his blood giving you that strength. Tomorrow we will have a transference ceremony to seal our marriage vows and your education can begin in earnest."

I smiled, but I wanted only to run away. I wanted to run as far and as fast as I could, and I wanted the old Todd to come with me. I remained glued to the sofa, my smile frozen in place, trying desperately to prevent the thoughts that were rolling around in my head from reflecting on my face.

"Society thinks we're murderers who slaughter unsuspecting innocent victims; sick people to be feared. But, they don't understand us. They don't understand how much we need them and they don't understand what we offer them in return. They don't understand how much of an honor it is to be selected for a transference ceremony. They have always, cruelly and unjustly, sought to wipe us out, constantly hounding us. One day we hope things will change for us.

"Ok. I'm done. I know I've only given you a broad sense of our community so far, but we wanted to give you the opportunity to ask us any questions you have at this point. We want you to feel comfortable and ask us about anything – anything at all—that feels unclear."

I thought, 'If *anything* was unclear? It was all unclear.'

I said, trying to buy some time to get my head around it all, "I just need some time by myself first, to absorb all that you've told me. I'd like to go upstairs for a little while or perhaps we can talk about it tomorrow."

"While I can understand how you must feel, it'll be better to get your initial questions out of the way now. It won't do much good to ruminate over it. Darling, why don't you stay here in the living room for a few minutes? We'll go out into the kitchen and you can call us when you're ready, but please don't take too long."

With that, Todd and the others got up and left me sitting in the living room. None of the others had anything to say to me as they left. They just walked out of the room. They didn't touch me in any way. They didn't even look at me. I was their daughter-in-law and his parents had no positive or soothing or encouraging or welcoming words for me. They had nothing to tell me, not even any stern warnings. They just walked out of the room. And these were the same people to whom Todd said he wanted me to ask any questions I had. Maybe that was their way, but I just couldn't comprehend how they could act like that to me or anyone else for that matter.

- 6 -

I had many, many questions, most of which I dared not ask. My first reaction was the same as what they said society thought about them, that they were murderers, that they were sick, and I'd add, that they were sad and deluded.

And what about Todd? How well he had hidden this from me, or *did* he give me clues, and I not see them, not want to see them perhaps. Perhaps he had been telling me, reaching out to me with his actions. I did not want to believe my husband a murderer. He did have a rip-roaring, practical-joking sense of humor, but he had always been a very kind and gentle-natured person. The Todd I knew did not jive at all with what he had just told me. I couldn't believe what he had told me. It was just too unimaginable to be real and I hoped that it wasn't real because if it was ...

It's true that he never really wanted to talk about his family and hadn't told me much about his life before he met me, but in the time I had know him he had done and said so many things that were the exact opposite of the person who could kill another human being in cold blood. From helping my elderly neighbor with her grocery bags, to patiently explaining and teaching things to people, to helping my friend set up her computer, to carrying me for over two miles when I injured my ankle while we were hiking last summer, Todd had always proven himself to be a caring and giving person.

My family and friends liked him, and thought he was very smart, hard working, personable, and funny. They were happy for me. They never mentioned sensing anything wrong or off about Todd to me, with the possible exception of my parents being troubled by the fact that neither they nor I had ever met his parents while we were dating. It bothered my parents that Todd would always politely rebuff them whenever they suggested inviting his family, especially his parents, over for dinner or to any of our family gatherings. But, they didn't feel it appropriate to interject themselves too deeply into my personal decisions.

I did not want to speak with his family or with anyone else right now. I only wanted to speak alone with my husband. What I wanted to talk to him about was between him and me, and was no one else's business. Besides, I did not get the feeling that Todd could tell me what I wanted to know with an audience listening in, pressing on him. And that in itself was odd. Todd was very dynamic and charismatic. That was part of his charm. He was also very bold, and with the possible exception of how he behaved around his community members, he had always exhibited a take-charge personality that people seemed to gravitate towards and rely on.

And he had been very loyal to me. I could always count on him to have my back. I felt at home with him and loved him right from the beginning of our relationship. Sometimes you just know when it's right and I loved him still and in spite of all that had just been thrown at me. I felt determined to get my arms around the situation and find a way through it for Todd and me, and I think, although he didn't come right out and say it in so many words, Todd wanted me to also.

I just couldn't believe, refused to believe, that Todd could have committed murder. Maybe, some of the others could. Maybe, some I hadn't met. But, not Todd. I wouldn't believe it unless he told me himself and even then, I couldn't be sure he wasn't making it up for some reason.

I was so antsy that I couldn't keep still. The way I was twisting and turning, and moving my arms and legs about, even as I remained seated on the sofa, would have made quite a show for someone if they had been looking in on me as I struggled with my thoughts.

Finally, no longer able to contain my energy, I got up and began pacing around the room. I don't know why, but I was always better able to think when I was moving around. But after a few minutes, the thought occurred to me that some of the others might very well have been spying on me the whole time without my knowledge or perhaps taking an occasional peek. Not wanting them to see me in this unruffled state, I sat back down, closed my eyes and took a few slow, deep breaths, and tried my utmost to put a tranquil veneer over my inner turmoil.

How was I going to convince the group to leave me alone with Todd? I tried to focus on figuring that out, mulling over the possibilities. How would I broach the topic? Would Todd support me in this request or side with the group and try to convince me to speak with everyone together as they wanted? I didn't think so. If I made my desire in that regard clear to him, he'd support me and find a way, his own way, to back me up. I was sure of it. Blood is thicker than water, but love is thicker than blood.

My mind drifted to his first wife, the wife who had rejected him and broken his heart, whose love had turned to revulsion when she learned his secret. I knew very little about her. Todd's mother seemed to have liked her well enough—well enough to pay her some indirect compliments on my wedding day, even though her former daughter-in-law had broken Todd's heart.

I was having a hard time believing all that I had heard. And why was I only hearing the story from Todd. Why didn't Emily and Malcolm offer any explanations, or his parents, or the nameless, frightening, cold-looking man who had stood behind Emily? It was all so confusing. According to Todd, his first wife was confused and *never* understood. I was determined to understand, hard as that seemed at this moment.

When after twenty minutes or so had gone by and I still hadn't called out to Todd and the others to come back into the living room, they took it upon themselves to return and check on me; all except for Todd.

As they filed past me, they were all palpably different. They gave off very soothing vibes and their faces, even the cold-looking man's, radiated warmth and sympathy. Todd's mother sat down next to me on the sofa.

"How are you doing, dear?" she asked. "Are you okay?"

I stared at her, dumbfounded, confused over her newfound concern and politeness.

"Where's Todd?"

"We sent him away to take care of something. He'll be back later tonight," his mother replied, as she placed the large manila portfolio that she was holding down onto the sofa beside her.

"What? Why didn't he tell me himself that he was leaving? Where did he go?"

"He wanted to, but we convinced him, with much difficulty, that it was better not to. We're sorry for this evening and—"

"Where is he?" I said, feeling both alarmed and increasingly impatient with everything that had transpired so far. My exhaustion was loosening my tongue.

Todd's father interjected, "That's not important. Don't worry. Everything's fine. We wanted to talk with you alone." The tone of his voice was flat as he uttered these words with a slow and deliberate forcefulness. He was trying to calm me, but his eyes belied his own anxiety over the situation.

"Like I was saying," his mother continued. "We're all very sorry for this evening and everything that you've been put through. Truly we are. But he's our son, and Emily and Malcolm's nephew, and for Todd's sake, we hope that we'll be able to trust and count on you."

"Why didn't any of you say anything to me before we got married? You said nothing at all to me. You knowingly let me believe things that weren't true," I blurted, looking from one to the other and then back again to his mother.

Visibly pained by my accusatory remarks, she proceeded to try as best she could to offer an explanation.

"We needed you to hear Todd's story from Todd himself. We felt that without first hearing what Todd had to say, you wouldn't believe, wouldn't want to believe what we have to tell you now. And you need to know about him ... need to understand about our son. As my husband said, we sent Todd away for a little while because we didn't want him to be present when we talked to you. We don't want him to know that we've spoken to you."

As she talked, I thought 'okay, so much for me talking alone with my husband. What's this new hurdle going to be?'

"Todd would never forgive us and you must understand that it could possibly do irreparable harm if he knew that you were aware of his illness— thought he was ill—and reacted to him that way. You must never let on that you know. Please. Because if you do tell him, talk to him about it, we are afraid that he will fall into a worse state than when his first wife left him. This time he might never recover. He loves you so much. We didn't feel we had the right to stop him from marrying. We hope though that in time you can forgive us for keeping you in the dark. We hoped that—"

"I don't know what to think anymore. I'm exhausted. My head's been bounced around from one end of the spectrum to the other, first by Todd,

now by all of you. Please, just tell me what's going
on. What's wrong with Todd?"

Emily got up and sat down on the other side of
me to try to bolster me up, and because Todd's
mother was also a bit overcome herself, with all that
she had just begun to reveal about their well-kept
family secret.

Todd's father, sparing his wife, picked up where
she'd left off. "Todd told you that we're ... well ...
essentially cannibals. Of course, he's not. We're
not. It's so sad, my poor son. It's a fantasy world he
has been building in his mind since junior high
school and this imaginary world of his has only
become more elaborate over time and more difficult
to manage.

"He was hospitalized for a while when he was
in high school, but neither therapy nor drugs seemed
to help him snap out of his dream world. Back then,
his symptoms were much milder. His fantasies were
all about success and making up stories about things
that never happened and not at all like what they've
progressed to today. He hated being in the hospital

and it made our usually outgoing and vibrant son terribly depressed. His doctors tried to show him that his fantasies were just that, fantasies, and not real. The more convincing they were, the more it seemed to break his spirit, and our hearts broke to see it. We couldn't bear watching it, especially his mom. We promised him we'd never send him back there."

To me, it seemed, there was no question about it. I said, "But if he's sick, sick in the way he seems to have become, he could end up hurting someone. He *should* be in the hospital."

"We can't do that to him," his father replied. "We love him too much. It would destroy him. But, I'm afraid, even though we've meant well, our not really knowing how to handle the situation has only added to the problem. In going along with his fantasies, we've had to create some very intricate set ups and ruses, sometimes going to great lengths to ensure that no one gets hurt. Our son has a very gentle nature, which has been the one saving grace all these years he's been ill. He's never had a desire or the heart or the willingness to do any killing himself, but lately he's begun beating himself up pretty badly over that perceived inability."

The only thing in my mind was, 'W*hat?* Was I really hearing all this.'

I shuttered to think what those ruses might be. Perhaps this evening and their behavior was one of those ruses. And what did he mean by ' he's never had a willingness or desire to do any killing himself'. I was fixated on that and had to ask, "Has *anyone* ever been killed or injured?"

Everyone remained silent, looking back and forth at each other, shocked and seemingly thrown off-guard by my question. Did they think I wouldn't ask?

"*Has anyone*?" I repeated more forcefully when I did not get an answer, asking my question directly to Todd's father.

"No.   Thankfully," he said, rather unconvincingly. I had no other choice though at this point than to take him at his word.

He shifted in his chair, then leaned forward, resting his forearm on his crossed leg, looking somewhat perturbed as if he was wrestling with what he wanted tell me next and trying to decide whether he should or not. He decided to plow ahead.

"Janie, Todd's first wife, felt she could not participate and even worse than that, she left him shortly after she found out about his illness. She's since remarried and Todd didn't take it very well when he found out about it. In fact, he took it quite hard. If she had moved away, perhaps it would have been easier. We don't think she told her second husband that she was married to our son though. At least he doesn't appear to know. He manages the gas station over in the next town.

"It took a long time for him to recover, but periodically coming here and seeing her only serves as a sad reminder. We try to keep him away from here, but Todd's very insistent. He's developed a bit of an obsession with her lately, trying to understand why she left him. Much to our dismay, he's started, more and more fervently, pursuing an answer from her, but nothing she has told him so far has satisfied him. It's gotten to the point where Janie has now implied to my wife that unless she ... we ... keep Todd away from her and get him to, as she put it, 'quit harassing her', she would get the police involved. She feels frightened by him—although there's really no need to be—and said that she just wants to be left alone. We haven't been able to convince our son to let things be.

"Janie always takes long walks in the woods, gathering information on birds and such for the books she writes, so a few weeks ago, Malcolm, me, and—"

"Enough about Janie. Time's getting short," Malcolm cut him off, half-yelling.

He seemed barely able to contain his anger at his brother. Todd's father didn't appear to agree. Nevertheless, he began describing other aspects of the situation. I didn't get the impression that Todd's father taking too long to tell the story was what had fueled Malcolm's anger.

None of the others spoke up, but out of the corner of my eye I thought I saw Todd's mother motioning to his father, with a couple of quick shakes of her head, to just let it go for now.

It must have been Todd's first wife Janie that I had seen in the restaurant earlier in the day. It had to have been. Todd didn't look sad when he saw her. Not even a little. And she didn't look annoyed to see him, like a fly constantly buzzing around her head that she was getting tired of swatting away. She looked scared, terrified actually. After all that I had heard, it troubled me that Todd could be so cool and calm about it with me when we were at the restaurant. He did not mention that she was his first wife, not even when I pointed the troubled woman out to him and he had turned around to look at her. He gave no indication that she was someone he knew. It had to be her though. It couldn't just have been a coincidence.

"Todd never took you home to see us and—"

"I want to know more about Janie and what happened with her and Todd," I interrupted.

The tension between Todd's father and Malcolm thickened.

"Another day we'll go into it. But, not now," Todd's father said. "There's much to tell you, but they are things that are best left for another day."

Belaboring the issue further wasn't likely to get me anywhere, so I dropped the subject. Maybe I could get Todd's father alone sometime. Todd's parents seemed a lot more forthcoming about things than his uncle Malcolm did. That was strange because I'd have thought it would have been the other way 'round.

"Alright," I said, acquiescing, and as Malcolm sat quietly assessing me, Todd's father continued.

"As I was saying, Todd never took you home to see us and up until now we've been pretty reserved with you. Once Todd feels you have fully adopted and accepted his world, we'll be able to talk normally with you in his presence. It's all part of Todd's fantasy world and we've had no choice but to play along with it in the hopes that we can keep his fantasies from getting away from our ability to contain them."

One more row of my beautiful sweater, my beautiful dream of happy ever after, unraveled.

"He loves you. He loves you very much. You mean the world to him," Todd's father said. "It is our hope that you'll understand and forgive him. He didn't deceive you. Not really. He couldn't help it. He was just following the rules of his fantasy world."

"If he's this sick," I said, repeating my previous observation, "he should be in the hospital. What if he starts fantasizing about something or does something that you can't, as you say, 'contain'?"

"Please. You must never suggest the idea of hospitalization to Todd," his mother implored, grabbing hold of my arm that was closest to her. "I fear what would happen." In her anxious state, her fingernails dug deep into my arm. Her fear pressed itself into my brain as well. Reflexively, I backed down and tried to reassure her.

"Don't worry. I won't suggest it. Things will work out okay," I said, not at all sure that they actually would.

Comforted a bit by what I had just told her, she removed her hand from my arm.

Emily, doing her best to be positive and trying to put a different spin on it, described a future that could be happy if only I'd let it be so.

"You love him as much as he loves you," she said. "I know you do. So it's not the marriage that you expected. What marriage is? What marriage doesn't have things, situations, that need to be overcome, accommodated? Don't let this bump in the road get in the way of your future happiness together."

I was puzzled by her equating this to the usual to-be-expected marital bumps in the road. This was a hill, not a bump, a big, steep, rocky hill to get over. A hill that they were all making more difficult to 'overcome' by inadvertently encouraging Todd's illness to flourish unchecked. Todd's father said that they try their best to contain it. But from what they told me already, their approach didn't seem to be working out very well.

I did love Todd, illness or no illness, but I did not want to lead a life of deception, did not want to look in my husband's face day after day and lie to him to keep his fantasy world intact. That was no way to live; constantly on edge; constantly walking on eggs shells; constantly in fear of what might happen next. And I did not want to be like poor Janie either.

Then everyone started at me, a chorus of hopefuls, coaxing and herding and corralling me into their life of deception; everyone except for the cold-looking man who had stood behind Emily before. He kept quiet until finally he could no longer do so.

"You all already know what I think. I've told you before, but none of you wants to hear it. Todd should be in the hospital. At least now, you're hearing it from someone else close to Todd. Bridget here agrees with me. Sorry, Bridget; I haven't introduced myself to you. I'm Jack Lester, a long-time friend of the family."

This was the man who just an hour before had stood behind Emily, stone-faced and unapproachable. They were all quite adept actors around Todd. I wondered what Jack's part was. Even Emily, with whom I had talked with quite a few times on the phone, never once mentioned to me that Malcolm was related to Todd, that he was Todd's uncle on his father's side. I was puzzled; why the charade about that? Why couldn't Todd just have said 'my aunt and uncle have a lake cabin they've offered to let us stay at for our honeymoon'?

Before I could say anything to Jack, Todd's father interjected. "That's out of the question. *You know that.* Why do you keep insisting on bringing it up?"

"Why is it out of the question?" I asked. "I mean if he's as sick as he seems to be, maybe you should all reconsider it."

"It's really not *that* bad," his mother said. "We hope in time, he'll snap out of it on his own, let go of his fantasy world."

"Until then we want him to know that we'll always support him," his father added, staring at Jack as he spoke. Jack argued the point no further.

He retreated into silence, but was still quite visibly in disagreement with how the others were handling the problem.

"Tell me," I said. "Does Todd realize that they're just fantasies? Has he ever given you any sign of that? Perhaps, some part of him realizes, but he just can't help himself, can't break free of them."

I was starting to try to get my arms around the problem, trying to get as much information as they were willing to give me.

"No," Malcolm said. "He really believes it whole-heartedly—at least as far as we can tell. He hasn't let on any differently. Janie suggested it to him and *that* did not go over very well. Todd told you a little bit about that himself earlier.

"And no one's ever mentioned anything to us about suspecting he was ill; not our friends; not our neighbors; not any acquaintances or strangers we've had casual dealings with; no one. No one outside our family and our close friend Jack here has ever indicated that they noticed anything was wrong. And we want to keep it that way, for Todd's sake."

I found it hard to believe that Todd and them would have been able to keep Todd's illness a secret for so long, that no one outside their inner circle had noticed or said anything about it.

"*No one* has said *anything* to Todd or to you about Todd that you know of?" I said in a mildly scolding tone. "I find that a bit hard to believe."

"Well, think about it. Did you *yourself* notice anything that would indicate that he was ill in the way that he is?" Malcolm shot back at me, trying to take me down off the heights he felt I was asking the question from.

I didn't respond, but he seemed to interpret and accept my non-response as a quiet apology for the upstart behavior I had just displayed.

We all talked for a while longer and then Todd's mother noted the time and indicated to the group that they should be going soon. We were all feeling rather spent from the stressfulness of the evening's events and I think neither they nor I were up to interacting with Todd again this evening, especially with all of us together. Todd's mother suggested we call it a night. There would be plenty of time in the coming days and months to discuss things further.

Still feeling distressed about the unsure territory I was in, I managed to convince them to stay just a bit longer. I knew so little and wanted them to tell me more—to help me better understand what was going on with Todd. They were reluctant to at first because they were worried that Todd would walk in and inadvertently overhear us discussing him. But in the end, they acquiesced.

At times, their explanations and opinions directly contradicted each others, making it difficult to know what to believe or to think. When I asked them what they thought was causing his fantasies or making them get more severe, I got responses that were all over the map.

Todd's mother and father, after much soul-searching and exploring of various possibilities, felt that his illness was a result of societal pressures, and that with time and love Todd would eventually be able to deal with those pressures in a more appropriate manner. Malcolm thought it was due to the usual childhood imaginings, which his parents had allowed to get out of control to the degree that Todd could no longer tell them apart from reality. He felt that there was nothing wrong with Todd that a good firm dose of reality wouldn't solve, something his brother and sister-in-law were reluctant to give him. Emily really didn't have a firm opinion on it, but based on what she had been reading lately, she was now thinking that perhaps it could be a chemical imbalance. And lastly, Jack Lester had no opinion. For him, all their opinions were irrelevant. The reasons didn't matter. Only Todd's actions mattered and his actions indicated that he should be under a doctor's care. It was the medical profession's job to figure out the best course of action for helping Todd to overcome his illness.

Once more, Todd's mother anxiously cautioned me against discussing or even mentioning the situation with anyone beyond those few that already knew. That could only bring more trouble and, most likely, would not end well.

The thought of that made me uncomfortable. I did not want to keep such a big secret from my family, even though I understood their reasons for requesting I do so. But, if I did tell my family or anyone else for that matter, I would be dragging them into this conspiracy of sorts and making them accomplices, and I did not want to do that either. The thought of that was worse than keeping it a secret. I would not be able to consult my family for advice. I suddenly felt completely isolated, alone with no sure, safe handle to grab onto for support.

I knew what they would have probably told me though. They thought Todd was a wonderful guy and were very happy that I was so happy, but they also thought that we hadn't know each other for a long enough time before we got married. But how long does it take to know when it's the right guy. I loved being with him. We had been so comfortable together, right from the start.

They also didn't like the idea that I never spent any time with his family before we got married, let alone that they didn't even get to meet them before our wedding. That didn't sit well with them either.

I could be wrong, but I think my family would have advised me to leave Todd, same as Janie had done. Even though the day's revelations had been a terrible shock and I had felt scared at times, I wasn't willing to do that. I loved him and I was still just as sure as ever that he loved me. But, I did wish I could contact my family to help me sort things out.

We all got up and started heading towards the door. I had Emily and Malcolm's cell phone numbers and his parents made sure I had theirs. Jack Lester didn't offer me his phone number and I didn't ask him for it. I wanted his number also, just in case, but my sense of propriety won out over my desire to obtain it.

Todd's mother handed me the manila portfolio she had kept next to her, and so closely guarded from the time they all re-emerged from the kitchen. She then proceeded to politely machine gun me with instructions concerning it. The portfolio contained some information that her and Todd's father had accumulated over the years, which might help me better understand Todd's illness. I was to make sure I put it somewhere where Todd would not find it and only look through its contents when I was sure he would not walk in on my doing so. The portfolio was not for me to keep—it was only a loan. And lastly, she hoped that I would be able to keep an open mind and heart as I studied the various papers and photos enclosed within it.

Emily, in her caring and encouraging way, tried to fortify me for the times ahead. "You're bright. I've no doubt that you'll be able to handle things. I have a good feeling about you. Todd's been so much happier since he's met you. I know both of you will get past this. You'll have a long life, children, and much happiness together."

As Emily made this last remark about children, I could see Malcolm rolling his eyes in disbelief, unable to fathom why Emily would bring up the idea of children *now*, even if just in passing.

Malcolm hurried everyone along and the others began to say their final goodbyes as well. I couldn't bring myself to ask when I'd see them again. They didn't mention anything about the ceremony that Todd said would occur tomorrow. Would they also be there? I didn't know. Was I supposed to go it alone with Todd? That was a possibility I did not want think about it.

I thought, 'Candlelight; romance; relaxing, sweet honeymoon days. Where did you go?'

Both of his parents gave me a hug, which I tentatively returned. Even though I understood the reasons for their prior behavior towards me, it was going to take me a while to become acclimated to this sudden switch from icy to warm. I wondered how they were going to react in the future when Todd was present. I wondered the same about myself.

I tried to push the myriad of thoughts and information just dumped on me from my mind. I needed to focus on what I was going to do right now, because Todd would be back shortly.

- 7 -

Todd and I needed to talk about what transpired this evening, but it had been one of the longest and most draining days I've ever experienced in my life so far, and I hoped never to have to live through that sort of day again.

My brain felt so fried. I didn't want to have even a casual conversation with him in that state. With the others gone, I could feel my body giving itself permission to conk out. Even though I felt wired, I could barely keep my eyes open any longer. Now was not the time to talk with Todd. Nothing good could come from having a conversation about important matters when you're overtired.

Tomorrow would be a better day to get to know more about this new side of Todd. So I went upstairs and stashed the portfolio far under the top end of the bed. It would be safe enough there until I could think of a more secure spot to keep it. I then hastily prepared for bed, hoping that if he found me sound asleep when he came home that he wouldn't have the heart to wake me—not that I expected to get a wink of sleep even though I felt completely wiped out.

I was wrong.

I was lying in bed, facing way from the bedroom door when I heard Todd coming up the stairs. The sound stopped when he was still—from what I could make out—in the hallway. I strained, my ears listening for the slightest sound, my body perfectly still, my mind willing the not-really-so-noisy wind outside to cease and desist.

Then I heard him moving again, and after a few seconds, sensed him standing over me, looking down at me.

I waited. I told myself, 'Don't move. Remember to breathe.' The undertow of deception was already tugging more and more forcefully at my ankle.

I waited. He was still hovering over me. I could feel him there. Fear rose up in me. Fear of my beloved husband. I shamed it and banished it from my being.

He gently touched my shoulder and stroked my hair. When I did not stir, he jostled my shoulder a bit harder. I remained completely still.

Finally. Relief.

Todd moved away and I could hear him quietly moving about in the semi-darkness, preparing for bed. It had been a long day for him too and possibly even more stressful than it had been for me, weighed down as he was, under all the uncertainty of how I would react. My reactions had not been negative or disdainful in any way. At least he hadn't seemed to interpret them that way. I hoped the small amount I managed to say earlier in the evening would be enough to sustain him until we could talk things out, and even though I knew it was for the best, I couldn't help feeling guilty about my decision to feign being asleep.

Gingerly, he slipped himself underneath the covers and laid there for a few moments without moving. He was facing towards me and I could feel the faintness of his breath against the back of my head and neck as he starting edging a little closer, not stopping until he was right alongside me, his head resting near my neck. I exhaled and closed my eyes tighter as a shudder uncontrollably rippled through my body, and I hoped he didn't feel it. In a barely audible voice, he whispered, "I love you, Bre. I love you," and then drifted off to sleep.

Sinking into a sad frame of mind, I tried to counter it by filling my head with positive images. I thought about the romantic walks on the beach Todd and I sometimes took, but it didn't help. I really needed to get some rest for what promised to be a long and tense next day. I commanded my disobedient, weary brain to shut down, but it wouldn't obey me, not for a long time—a really long time. After I felt surer that Todd was asleep, by some miracle, I was finally able to fall asleep myself.

- 8 -

When I opened my eyes the next morning, Todd was still asleep. He looked so peaceful. I lay there, using the time to think of what to do next, thinking of what to say.

But what could I say? Should I totally immerse myself in his fantasy world, not that I knew what all the rules of it were? Perhaps say, 'Good morning, darling. Did you sleep well? Have some of the delicious cheese-covered fingers that I've prepared especially for you for breakfast.' And then proceed to serve him some make-believe, yet real-looking fingers? Did I have that much imagination? I was sure my anemic out-of-shape imagination was no match for his. And I couldn't say or do things like that anyway. I would feel like I was mocking him.

Perhaps I should be direct and say, 'Why did you lie to me?' Then when he looked back at me, all shocked and hurt, say, 'Yes. You did lie by not telling me anything about it the whole time we were dating and not even telling me about it after we got engaged.'

What should I say? I had no idea.

Should I tackle the situation head on or should I bide my time, and go slow, taking my cues from Todd's actions?

I had slept some at least, but I was still tired.

It seemed the best thing for me to do at this point was to proceed with caution and learn what I needed to know one morsel of information at a time, and after obtaining enough of those small fragments, hopefully the right path to take would eventually become clear to me.

The one thing I knew already was that I wasn't going to leave Todd, scary as his illness was. If the tables were turned, he would be there for me. He wouldn't just abandon me when he found out. Of that, I was sure. And I loved him. I wanted to spend the rest of my life with him.

As Emily said, we would find a way to get past what she had called a 'bump in the road' that was really a hill.

I fell back asleep for a while and when I woke up again, Todd was gone. Figuring that he was probably downstairs, I got up and decided to use this small window of opportunity to call my parents in private. This way I could avert any potential questions Todd might have about my conversation with them, not to mention avoiding the possibility of him mentioning the call to his family, who might then wonder whether I had perhaps revealed any of their confidences against their wishes.

My parents weren't expecting a call from me until tomorrow and even though they were aware of where we were going on our honeymoon—they had the address and a copy of the directions—I was feeling so anxious about everything that I wanted someone to keep tabs on me, at least a little bit.

My handbag was still where I had left it yesterday, on the dresser. However, when I fished around in it for my cell phone, I couldn't find it. It's not that big of a bag and I can usually find my cell phone rather quickly. Now that I was in a hurry, of course it figured that I would have a problem locating it. I dumped the contents of my handbag out onto the bed—gum, my wallet, tissues, hairbrush, and everything else, but my cell phone.

The last time I had used it was in the restaurant the day before to call my girlfriend Nancy, while I was waiting for Todd. I'm very careful with my phone and am not one to leave it lying about, and when I'm out of the house, I always put it back in my handbag immediately after I use it. I was positive I did that when I used it last, but I guess there's a first time for everything.

So now, we only had Todd's phone, unless mine eventually turned up. Emily had mentioned to me, the first time we talked on the phone, that the cabin had no landline. They only used their cell phones whenever they were there.

If I was going to make a call, I'd have to use Todd's phone, and I had no choice but to use it with his knowledge because he had secured his with a lock code, the same as I did with mine. He'd either have to tell me what the code was or unlock it himself before giving the phone to me.

I called down the stairs to Todd because I wanted to let him know that I was up and would be down in a short while after I showered and dressed, but I got no reply, even after I called out to him again a little louder. Thinking he was just out of earshot, I decided to skip the shower and quickly washed my face, brushed my teeth, pulled my hair back into a ponytail, and put on my clothes. I also put on my sandals. Walking around the house in my bare feet, which is the most comfortable way for me, didn't seem like the prudent thing to do under the circumstances.

Expecting that Todd would probably be in the kitchen, I looked for him there first, but he wasn't there. Our car was still visible from the kitchen window, so I knew that he had to be around somewhere close by. After searching around inside a bit more, I finally found him outside on the front deck, his hands outstretched on either side him on the railing, looking out at the lake, lost in thought.

"Morning!" I said cheerfully, walking over to where Todd was standing.

Todd turned to look at me, a happy-to-see-me smile instantly forming on his face. He then turned his head back in the direction of the lake.

"It's great out today. Smell that air," he said, taking in a huge lungful. "You were sleeping so soundly when I woke up that I didn't want to wake you." When I reached where he was standing, he put his arm around my shoulder and gave me an enthusiastic kiss hello.

I tilted my head back, closed my eyes, and breathed deeply.

"It's our honeymoon. We deserve a little rest and relaxation," he said. "Hell. We can sleep 'til noon if we feel like it. No alarm clocks this week!" His spirits were high; the weight he had been carrying around was gone.

"C'mon in the kitchen," I said, coaxing him toward the door. I peeled myself away and pulled on his hand. "I'll make us some breakfast. I thought I noticed they had a box of oatmeal. I can cook you some of that if you like. You want scrambled eggs?"

I was not going to talk about yesterday, at least not just yet, unless he brought it up. Besides, he looked so optimistic and full of life that I couldn't bring myself to mention it.

"Hmm. Let's see ... oatmeal with raisins and brown sugar ... and some scrambled eggs. I'm so hungry this morning," Todd said, as he began to set the table.

I rolled my eyes in my mind, trying not to even think about the rest of *that* expression that popped into my head. I put up the coffee, got the oatmeal started, and then began working on the eggs. Todd opened and closed the upper cabinet doors, looking for the raisins and the brown sugar.

"I know they're around here somewhere. Emily's big on raisins." He found the raisins. "One down," he said, and continued on his quest for the sugar. "They have so much stuff in these cabinets ... Yes! Found it."

Casually, as I divvied up the oatmeal and the eggs, I said, "I noticed this morning that my phone's gone missing. I know I had it yesterday in the restaurant."

"It's not missing. It's over there on the far counter," Todd said, pouring me some orange juice and tossing his head in the direction of where my phone was. "I'm charging both our phones." I didn't know if I liked the idea of him rummaging around in my handbag. That was something he never did before, at least not to my knowledge, but I let it go. I had been so focused on finding my phone when I emptied my handbag's contents on the bed that I hadn't even noticed that the charger was missing also.

"Great! Thanks. You always think of everything."

Todd's eyes twinkled at my show of appreciation, and he motioned to me to keep going as I spooned the oatmeal into his bowl. I was glad I made extra.

The quiet, peacefulness of the lake, which had seemed so wonderfully rejuvenating the day before, was now unnerving. I wanted some noise, some distraction, to help take the focus off the two of us. We had a leisurely breakfast, but conversation was difficult. Even so, I managed to keep pace with Todd and chatted about this and that, and nothing too heavy; things like too bad we didn't have the morning paper because I missed reading through it, maybe we could go antiquing this week, or on a nature walk, or perhaps, go bird watching.

That last suggestion was my first mistake. I kicked myself for bringing up bird watching, his first wife's interest, but he didn't seem troubled by the mention of it. She was ever-present in the back of my mind and thoughts of her situation were seeping out in odd ways.

Scooping up a large forkful of eggs, Todd said, "I used to come here all the time, growing up. There's a small clubhouse that my brother and I built

one summer that's not too far away from the cabin.
I'll show it to you if you like."

When we were planning our honeymoon, he
didn't even know Emily and Malcolm. Last night I
learned that Malcolm was his uncle. Now, it seems,
he used to come here, to their cabin by the lake, all
the time. Was anything he told me true, or rather—
real? He didn't seem to remember what he had told
me before.

I didn't remind him that yesterday afternoon we
discussed taking the boat out to sail over to some of
our neighbors to see if they were there and let them
know that we were staying at the cabin for the week
and to get acquainted with some of them.

"That'd be nice. I'd like to see the clubhouse
you and your brother built. And it'll give us
something to do. There's not much to do around
here. I'm not used to so much relaxation."

I'm not a liar. I always valued the fact that
Todd and I had a very open and honest relationship.
Maybe he was being honest with me, in his way, and
all this was just a part of his illness. Hard as it was,

I could understand that—if that was the case. But what about me? Here I found myself placating Todd, which in my book amounted to the same thing as lying. I hated that.

"Yea. Me neither," he agreed. "But, it is nice to unwind. I can think of something else for us to do," he said, reaching over to me and planting a series of kisses on my neck and shoulder."

"You read my mind," I said. I got up and started clearing the dishes off the table and carrying them over to the sink. "Gonna help me?" I teased.

"I'm beginning to rub off on you, I see. Quite the jokester you are this morning." I winked my reply.

The more time passed with no mention of the prior evening's revelations from Todd, the more difficult it became not to ask about it. Those revelations had come from out of nowhere. I didn't know if or when another one would come crashing into me. He had never displayed any signs or given me any indication that he was ill, that I could recall, but I confess I never really looked at things as microscopically as I was now starting to.

He was as sweet and gentle as ever; and so happy. That was the hard part. I was afraid to bring things up I guess.

As Todd and I were cleaning up in the kitchen, I remembered the portfolio his mother had given me the night before. I wanted to look through it, in hopes that it would give me some clues about how to best proceed and shed more light on the man I married and used to think I knew all about. If I was going to help my husband, I needed to gather all the information I could get my hands on. But how was it going to be possible for me to have enough time alone to study the contents of the portfolio?

Todd took a break from bringing the rest of the dishes over to the sink, drumming on the edge of the countertop with his fingers, as he started to sing a tune, making up the words as he went along, "Sweet, sweet, Bridget. Lovely as can be. Sweet, sweet Bridget. The only one for me. Loved you from the first and I'll love you foreeevverrrr—"

"Hey. Rest of the dishes," I broke in.

"—She's a songstress, par excellence. Her lyrics, sublime. She can conjure magical words. Wrap you in a spell. Baa dup bup bup bup." he continued, not paying attention.

He kept on cajoling me into singing along with him, but as much as I loved singing with him, or use to love singing with him, I just wasn't in the mood. My brain was fixated on the portfolio. After a short while of me—politely as I could—rebuffing him, he stopped, and once the rest of the dishes were cleared off the table, Todd retreated into the living room, leaving me at the sink to finish up.

Perhaps I could send him into town on an errand. No. He'd probably ask me to come along with him. What excuse could I give for staying behind? Feign fatigue or a sudden headache? Nah. Too lame and not really believable. I didn't get headaches very often. I never, in my wildest dreams, thought I'd be wishing that that wasn't the case. I couldn't think of a single thing that I thought would work. My only hope was that an opportunity

would present itself.   It finally did, later that
morning.

- 9 -

After breakfast, we went for a walk around the property and Todd showed me the clubhouse that he said he and his brother Craig had built when they were growing up. It wasn't too far away, but it was in the opposite direction from which we had walked the day before.

When we came upon the clubhouse, my jaw dropped, to Todd's delight.

Todd strolled around the outside of it, pointing to and describing the various parts of it that he was particularly proud of.

"I had wanted to expand it. There's plenty of room to do that, especially over on the other side, but we never ended up making it bigger. It's great though. Isn't it?"

My eyes darted around, taking everything in. "Absolutely," I said, nodding my head for emphasis. Todd walked back towards the front of the structure.

"You built this all by yourselves?"

"Just us. Of course, we didn't get the materials and tools ourselves, but the labor was all ours." Todd pointed up to the shingled roof. "I broke my arm falling off a ladder when we were doing the roof. Craig was playing around, shaking the ladder, and I lost my balance. I landed wrong. I didn't tell my parents about him shaking the ladder. They would have punished him."

I was happy Todd was beginning to open up more about his past.

"Your brother likes to clown around like you do."

"Yea. Guess so. We were pretty tight growing up. Don't really see each other that much nowadays though."

I had envisioned something relatively small, pieced together with wooden odds and ends, no windows, and a padlocked, makeshift door and dirt floor. Todd's clubhouse, although somewhat weathered and aged, was a miniature version of his aunt and uncle's well-adorned cabin. The clubhouse was replete with a slew of gadgets and features that the two brothers could spend hours and hours occupying themselves with—a microscope, games, water pistols, swimming gear, and lots of other items. It had paned glass windows, and a regular door and lock (*which Todd apparently had the key for on his key ring*), and its one room was very much larger than I expected.

It definitely didn't look to me like something that the boys would have built by themselves. I was going to ask him how old they were when they built it, but then decided against it. I didn't want to start sounding like a detective grilling a suspect. Todd was very handy, so who knows, maybe he and his brother really did build it themselves.

On the walls, and interspersed with the other objects, were some disturbing items that definitely called attention to Todd's obsession. And there were other seemingly normal items that you might expect to find in a country house, but in light of the previous nights eye-opening disclosures, they were rather worrisome to find there, including a three-pronged spear, knives, ropes, and a large slingshot.

There were a number of drawings tacked to the walls. I couldn't take my eyes off the largest one, attached to the far wall, and positioned high up so that its menacing image looked down on the viewer, its magic marker colors, dark and vibrant. It was as mesmerizing as it was ghastly. It depicted a young male cannibal with a fierce expression, head bent back, and a torn piece of bloody flesh jutting out of the corner of his mouth, the prey's still attached forearm tightly gripped in the cannibal's hand, the savaged body in front of where he was kneeling.

Most gruesome of all was that it appeared that the victim was still alive. A likeness of the clubhouse was in the distance.

"That's a drawing I did of Craig, you're looking at."

I had to force myself to speak and take my eyes off the drawing.

"He looks older. Not a boy."

"That's right. I drew it a few years ago."

I thought cannibals ate other humans as part of their rituals, but I didn't think that they were unnecessarily savage or brutal in their behavior towards their victims, and I didn't think they viewed it as a sport. They did what they did out of their belief system and not because they enjoyed it. But I didn't really know very much about it except from the little bit we had discussed rather quickly in one of my anthropology classes, and I didn't remember much about it.

The drawing made the cannibal (his brother) seem particularly mindless and violent, as if driven by pure instinct, but the drawing also had an undertone to it, as if the cannibal was relishing what he was doing. The man he was ripping apart was not a ritualistic sacrifice. It was his prey.

"He seems to be enjoying his meal."

"I don't think so. At least that's not what I intended. I enjoy drawing, but I'm no Rembrandt. I did most of these drawings with thin magic markers, so perhaps that's why they came out the way they did. It's hard to get very detailed and there's no erasing. I was going more for the feeling rather than realism."

He moved over to one of his other drawings.

"Wait," I said. "I'm curious. Who's the other man in the drawing? Anyone in particular?"

"No; no one in particular. It's just a man."

I studied it some more and then moved over to the other smaller drawing that Todd was now standing in front of. In this drawing, Todd had captured a very different feeling.

It was also of a cannibal, but this one was in the process of stirring a large pot. The top of a head with the hair still attached and various appendages and vegetables were sticking up out of the water, here and there. And he was sad. No, not sad; it seemed more as if he was forlorn. This cannibal didn't relish what he was doing.

"Cannibalism isn't an easy way of life," Todd said. "It can be quite difficult. In order to be a truly respectable cannibal, you need to have the killer instinct. You can't think deep thoughts or feel any empathy. You need to be sly and slick and you need to remain focused on the goal you're trying to achieve with your victim's sacrifice. And it's an honor to be selected, although most don't seem to feel at all honored."

"Who's the man in the drawing?"

"No one in particular; it's just a man."

"The drawings are so life-like," I said. "You're a very talented artist."

Todd grimaced. "Hardly. I do okay, but I wouldn't say that I'm a 'talented artist'. I do like drawing though. It's very different from overseeing large-scale computer system implementations; very relaxing; soothing almost. It's kind of a passion of mine."

"Have you shown them to anyone else?" I was curious because I had certainly never seen him draw anything. He never spoke about it, and I couldn't recall ever seeing any non-commercial artwork on display at his house, but then I hadn't gone there very often. It was one more thing that he did when I wasn't with him that I was just now finding out about.

"Nah. I never showed anyone my drawings. Besides these few, I keep most of them in a trunk back home and no one comes down here to the clubhouse anymore. Not even my brother. Not since we were kids."

I bit my tongue and let it go. I didn't ask him—as much as I really wanted to—why he never told me about his passion for drawing. Don't be negative, I reminded myself, that won't help things any.

His happy mood from just a short while ago was beginning to spiral downward. I wanted to hear more, but even more than that, I didn't want him to start becoming depressed. All that I was seeing only convinced me even more that he should be in the hospital or at the very least, under a doctor's care, but his parents were dead set against it and they had more familiarity with his illness and the history of it than I certainly did.

I reminded myself not to press things, to take slow steps.

"We should go. You can show me more of the clubhouse later. I'd love to see more of it and hear more about it. We were just going to have a quick peek and then go sunbathing down by the lake this morning. It's already 9:30. What do ya say? Shall we head back to the cabin?"

"Sure. Sure. Okay."

He was still looking at the drawing. I started for the door and he followed shortly after and locked it behind him.

The night before as Todd was talking, I felt frightened; so frightened that, at one point, I wanted to run as far away as I could get, as fast as I could— even though I loved Todd, in spite of what he was saying. Oddly, now, that feeling of fright had dissipated. Logically, I knew I should still be feeling that way and perhaps left—gone back home, together with Todd, or to someplace else that was safer than staying at the cabin—and dealt with the situation in a less isolated environment.

But being there was part of Todd's fantasy and who knows what would have happened if I suggested leaving. He'd have thought I didn't trust him or was afraid. I had no reason to go back home, except if there was an emergency. Anyway, if I had suddenly expressed a desire to leave, it might have triggered something worse, like what happened with his first wife.

I wasn't as frightened as I would have thought I'd be. I guess because I didn't really believe Todd—ill as he was—could do anything to hurt me. He loved me. He couldn't hurt anyone else either for that matter. I was so sure of that. My body, on the other hand, was reacting sometimes as though it was still scared and I resolved to try to keep those reactions at bay as much as possible.

When we were about halfway back to the cabin, I stopped and just stood there staring at him. Todd sensed what I was going to say, and before I could speak, he took my hand and squeezed it.

"I love you Todd. I want you to be happy. I want us to be happy together."

"I love you too," he said, wrapping his arms around me, "so much, so very much." He tightened his embrace and speaking directly into my ear, he whispered, "You're the warmest, most encouraging person I've ever met. You make me feel like I can do anything."

I pulled away from him so that I was staring directly into his eyes, and in a caring, drill-sergeanty voice, said, "You're brilliant. You can do anything you put your mind to. I know you can."

We went the rest of the way back up to the cabin to change into our sunbathing attire.

- 10 -

There was a floating wooden platform about forty yards from the dock. It served as a sun deck and diving platform. We figured we'd row over and stretch out on it for an hour or two and get some sun.

We could have also used the lounge chairs we rested on the day before, but we opted for the platform because it wasn't stationary and gently bobbed around in the water, making it even more relaxing than the lounge chairs. And we'd have full sun no matter which way we turned.

In nothing flat, Todd changed into his faded, blue denim cut-off shorts and flip-flops, removed his shirt, and then ventured into the hallway in search of some large towels we could lay on.

His phone rang. It was a work associate of his. I could tell—muffled as his voice was coming from down the hall—from bits and pieces of his side of the conversation. "The file should be on the L drive in the Winters directory … Yes. We'll need eleven … No … No, that shouldn't be a problem. Don't worry about it. I'll take care of it when I return … Okay, then just tell him that I told you eleven is more than sufficient … Yeah … Sorry, they put you in the middle. Okay. I'll give him a call …"

Ten minutes later, Todd came back into the bedroom, two oversized towels in hand.

"Ah! You found them. Great!"

"They were on the top shelf in the hall closet near the bath." He unfolded one, dangling it so I could see how big it was. I nodded my approval.

"That was work on the phone."

"Even on your honeymoon they call you! I hope they appreciate how conscientious you are."

"It was no big deal," Todd said, plopping himself on the bed, waiting for me to finish up. He leaned back on his elbows and glancing at my attire, grinned at me. I had decided to put on my two-piece green and white swimsuit—Todd's favorite—and matching cover-up.

"What? No itsy bitsy teeny-weeny yellow polka dot bikini? I don't know if I want to go sunbathing with a gal who's not wearing a yellow polka dot bikini!" he said in a mockingly serious tone of voice, and then eagerly awaited my response.

Normally, I would have said something like, "Okay. Well then I'll see you when I get back," smiled, and then crooked my finger at him, beckoning him to come over and kiss me an apology. But, I didn't say anything for some reason and I didn't crook my finger. I just pretend-pouted, then smiled.

I transferred my phone, a tube of suntan lotion, and some other items into an empty tote bag I had brought along, gave my hair a quick brush, and retied it into a ponytail, then stopped to think if I'd forgotten anything.

"All ready?" Todd asked me, seeing me standing, tote in hand, looking around the room.

Something to drink!

"We should fill up a bottle with some water perhaps," I said, heading towards the stairs.

"Hey. Didn't you forget something?"

"No. I don't think so."

Todd pointed to my flung-off sandals lying near the bed and started to bend down to pick them up. I scooted over to them, scooping them up before he had a chance to, banging him accidently with the tote bag in the process.

I slipped them on and made a sympathetic gesture towards my feet that were now prisoners once again.

"I'm married to a nut," Todd said, teasing, and shaking his head.

The last thing I wanted to deal with was Todd catching a glimpse of the portfolio stashed under the bed and making a comment about it. He probably wouldn't have noticed it at all—I had pushed it pretty far into the middle of the bed. But, even if he had noticed it, he probably would have thought it was just some personal stuff of Emily and Malcolm. It was a chance, however, that I didn't want to take.

Todd hurried down the stairs, ahead of me, taking the steps two at a time as he often liked to do. He was very agile. He was already by the sink, filling a bottle up with some water, by the time I came down the stairs and reached the kitchen. He capped the bottle, dropped it into the tote bag I was holding, then took it from my hand and carried it as we went outside, and down the short pathway to the dock.

———

The sun felt warm and wonderful on my face, and it was such a beautiful day out that it was easy to forget our current difficulties. And if truth be told, I guess somewhere in the back of my mind I wanted—no, needed—a bit of a break from the reality of it, at least for a little while.

Yesterday, when we were outside, there did not seem to be anyone around—at least within view—

but today there were some people out on the lake, boating. From the sundeck we were laying on, I could see our nearest neighbor, a middle-aged man, sitting at the far side of his deck, reading.

"Hello," I called out to him. "Hello, there." He raised his head briefly and turned in my direction, and I threw him a friendly wave. He did not acknowledge me. Probably hearing someone calling out, but unable to zoom in on where the sound was coming from, he just went back to his reading.

We had been luxuriating on the floating platform for about an hour, relaxing and having a good time, when Todd turned over onto his stomach, propped himself up on his elbows, and started staring out at the lake, becoming totally lost in his thoughts.

When I opened my eyes again sometime later, he was still in the same position. Even though the sun felt good, it was deceptively strong and looking down at my suntan-lotion-covered shoulders, I could see a slight tinge of red, so I put my cover-up on.

"Getting hungry?" I asked. "I am."

I got no response. He didn't hear me.

I nudged him. Todd looked over at me, only half-listening, and obviously still deep in thought.

Even though it worried me, I didn't ask him what he had been so lost in thought thinking about. I guess part of me was still apprehensive about what his answer would be. Battling my own denial, a secure and seductive refuge, was going to be just as arduous as helping Todd get well.

"Starting to feel hungry?" I asked again, getting up and proceeding to fold my towel. "C'mon. Let's go back and make some lunch."

"Sure. Alright," he replied, taking the towels from me.

We travelled in silence most of the way back, but just as we were approaching the front deck of the cabin, Todd tentatively asked, "Would you mind if I went into town for a little while after we eat? I won't be long."

I should have felt happy—or at least, relieved— because here he was presenting me with the perfect opportunity to study the contents of the portfolio that were waiting for me under the bed. But, now, since he wanted to go into town without me, I wanted to go along. I didn't really want to go along, but I wanted to know why he wanted to go alone. What was he planning on doing in town—alone? I didn't know how to pose the question though without it sounding accusatory.

"I'll come along. Maybe we can stop somewhere, pick up a newspaper, and take a walk around town."

"We can do that tomorrow ... and go antiquing like you wanted to. I'll see what newspapers they have and bring one or two back for you. You stay here. I won't be long—an hour, hour and a half, tops."

"But—"

"I have a surprise for you. Don't spoil it, Bre."

Todd knew that I loved it whenever he'd surprise me with some gift, something he saw and thought would please me, make me smile. And I did love the out-of-the-blue surprises he'd sometimes give me. Like the time he saw me admiring some imaginatively done glass figurines of different types of animals and then a week later surprised me with miniature glass giraffes—a whole family of them.

So, yes, I *used* to love surprises. But, yesterday's shocker was more than enough to cure me of that.

"You don't have to buy me flowers," I said in a momentary burst of hope, wishing it *was* a normal, everyday-kind-of-surprise he was planning. I knew it probably wasn't though.

"No. It's nothing like that. I'm positive that you'll be both delighted and awed. But, you're just going to have to wait and see what it is. You're not going to get me to tell you."

"I'm already awed … by you," I said, putting my arm around his waist and kissing him. "I don't need any gifts. You're the only present I want today." I stopped him from walking on and pulled him closer, looking at him in as fetching a way as I could, trying to get him to forget about his plans for a surprise.   "Let's just stay here this afternoon," I cooed.

And I thought I did manage to get him to forget. But, if I did, it was not for long.

After lunch, I was in the bathroom, when I heard him calling out to me, "Bye, Bre.   See you later."   He was already in the car and starting to drive away by the time I got to the door.

I dreaded the thought of what his surprise might be.   Trying to think of happy, harmless, small-scale possibilities, I imagined that he probably saw something nice in a store window the day before, on his way back to the café, and went into town to buy it for me—a sexy negligee or a pretty top or a pendant.   That's all.   But, then again, he did say 'awed', and while a pretty top was a nice gift, I didn't think it would *awe* anyone.

I was driving myself nuts ruminating over what he could be planning as a surprise, restlessly pacing about, as I did whenever I was anxious, for over a quarter of an hour.   Finally, I calmed down.   Todd was gone, so there was nothing I could do about it now. I'd have to wait and see what it was. I clung to the thought that it really would be something happy and awesome.

Upstairs, the portfolio awaited me, so I thought that I might as well use the time I had until Todd got back to look through it and learn whatever I could.

- 11 -

Before digging into the portfolio, I first reached out to my parents. They were not expecting me to call until tomorrow, but I didn't know when I'd get another opportunity to speak with them alone, and even more than that, I wanted to hear their voices—a comforting reminder of normalcy. I still had the feeling of wanting someone I knew and trusted to keep tabs on me. I felt like I was out there floating on my own, in unsure territory, with no sense of what direction to head, groping around blindly for the right path to take.

Like any family, we had our share of good times, occasional fights, and family troubles of one sort or another, which we always managed to get through. There was the tenacious, difficult-to-diagnose infection my younger brother, Brodie, caught on one of our family vacations; my long-time high school boyfriend breaking up with me during our first year of college; and the fire that demolished the entire back part of our home. Hard as these things had been to overcome, they seemed straightforward in comparison with what I was currently facing. I felt completely ill equipped to handle the situation.

His parents were not making it any easier by refusing to take him to the hospital, or even to a psychiatrist, and putting the fear into my head of what would happen to Todd if I did. They had put me in a terrible position by insisting I promise not to speak about Todd's illness with anyone, not even with my family. They seemed so certain that it was imperative I not do so (for Todd's sake). I was starting to feel sorry I gave them my word not to.

―――

My mom picked up the phone and was happy and excited to hear from me. Her love reached out to me, easing the rattling of my nerves. It was wonderful to be talking with her, even if it was from far away. My father was at home, but not my younger brother. She yelled out to my father, "Matt, our girl's on the phone," and I could hear his heavy footsteps hurrying towards her. "How's my girl?" he asked, taking the phone from my mother and then putting it on the speaker setting so that we could all talk together.

"We're okay," I blurted, and then reconsidering, "We're having a marvelous time here. It's so wonderful to hear your voices."

For a few minutes, we chatted about generalities. Everyone was well; the trip to the cabin was uneventful, no traffic; the cabin and lake were spectacular; and the washing machine my parents ordered arrived and dad had already hooked it up. The conversation was going along well until my mom happened to ask an innocent question—how our first evening at the cabin had been.

I hesitated. My brain was at a standstill, with no possible answers tossing around it, just a loud panicky static. On the job, I was quick on my feet when responding to unexpected customer issues, problems, and the occasional verbal attack; always nimble and able to come up with a workable solution or plan. Why was this question so difficult? I wanted to tell them everything, get their advice, but in doing that, I would be putting them into the middle of it. I couldn't do that to them. Firecrackers, dozens of them, all going off at the same time, replaced the static in my head.

I pushed and whipped my brain and after a several excruciatingly long moments, I haltingly replied, "We didn't do anything much. We just hung out, relaxing, listening to some music; just a nice, quiet, romantic evening." I thought, 'good grief! I couldn't come up with a better answer?'

"You sound funny, sweetheart. Are you sure that everything's okay?" my father asked. The joyful tone in his voice had turned to concern.

"Yes. Yes. I'm fine. Probably just a little tired from all the excitement of the wedding and then the drive up here. That's all."

My answer did little to vanquish the warning signs detected by my mother's razor-sharp intuition and now *both* of my parents were intently focused on the flashing radarscope blip labeled Bridget, "You didn't have an argument or anything with Todd did you?" she asked, ready to provide advice.

"All couples argue on occasion. Get everything out in the open.   Remember, Bridget, small, inconsequential disagreements have a tendency to mushroom into something more than what they were, if allowed to fester. It's always best to talk through any disagreement and put it to bed."

"We didn't have a fight. Everything is fine, ma!   Really it is ... We're thinking of going antiquing tomorrow. We passed some interesting places yesterday on the way here. Maybe, I'll find the lamp you've been looking for," I said, recovering and trying hard to change the topic and stop them from worrying about something being wrong. That was my second mistake.

I don't know if I was successful in allaying their concerns, but they didn't pursue it any further except to let me know that they both loved me and were there for me if I needed them. We talked for another two or three minutes and then said our goodbyes, and I asked them to give my love to Brodie and told them that I would call them again when we returned home from our honeymoon. If I had said I'd call any sooner than that, I figured they'd start worrying about me in earnest and I didn't feel right about doing that to them.

After the call, I remained sitting at the edge of the bed for a few moments, and then collapsed backward onto the bedspread. I lay there, staring at the perfectly painted ceiling, my eyes lazily tracing the molding and intricate patterns made by various hues of beige, working up the courage to fetch the portfolio from under the bed. Even though that was why I came up to the bedroom in the first place and what I really still wanted to do, I procrastinated for another few minutes. Then after having re-kindled my courage a bit, I got down and half lying on the floor, threw my arm underneath the bed and fished around for the portfolio, but it was not within reach. In my haste, I had shoved it too far under.

I lowered myself completely onto the floor alongside the bed and peered underneath the overhanging covers, in order to locate it. Seeing where it was, I tried to grab hold of it, but my arm was not long enough, nor my grasp strong enough to easily retrieve it. I stretched my arm as far as it would go and with the tips of my fingers, I wiggled the portfolio towards me, inch by inch, until it was close enough so that I could get my hand around it and pull it out.

Not taking anything out, I first thumbed through the portfolio to get a sense of what was inside. It contained an assortment of items— writings, drawings, news clippings, photographs, and articles, some from magazines, others printed off the internet. There was a set of papers at the back of the portfolio, a log held together with a binder clip, which listed different dates along with handwritten notes related to those dates. A few of the dates had single or double red asterisks next to them.

There didn't seem to be any doctor's reports or papers from Todd's short hospital stay during high school, and I hoped that there would at least be some details about it in the log.

I pulled out the first few items. They were drawings similar to the ones Todd had shown me in the morning—some sadder, some more gruesome. Replacing them back into the portfolio, I next pulled out a set of articles and news clippings. I was trying to be very careful about keeping everything in order, also making sure to not to have too much out at once, just in case Todd came back earlier than expected and I had to hide everything again in a hurry.

The articles and news clippings spanned a variety of themes including obsessive-compulsive disorders, cannibalism, different case studies, and stories about people with fantasy-prone personalities, fear and anxiety disorders, and various therapies. Others were about famous people with related conditions and/or natures. Glancing at the headlines and opening paragraphs, they appeared to be about these people's great achievements, describing how their natures benefitted rather than harmed them.

Many of the documents had annotations, underlined passages, and some were in bad shape, faded or worn. I pictured his folks, reading and re-reading some of the articles, desperate to find an answer and hoping that by reading the articles yet another time, the solution would somehow become apparent.

I wished I had enough time to study the information contained in the articles, but there was only enough time to skim through them before Todd returned. Other items in the portfolio might possibly contain information that was more critical for me to be aware of and I wanted to get a better sense of what they were. If possible, I'd read the articles later. The research his parents had done would certainly be of tremendous help in giving me a head start, but I intended to do my own research when we returned home anyway.

Almost forty-five minutes had passed since Todd left. After scolding myself for not doing a better job of budgeting my time, I decided to skip to the log file at the end of the portfolio. I really should have looked at it first instead of starting at the beginning and working my way to the back, but there was nothing I could do about it now.

Interestingly, the first date in the log was from when Todd was five years old. His kindergarten teacher had made mention of the fact that Todd was always daydreaming. Throughout the rest of his elementary school years, his teachers gave him low marks for following instructions (he had a tendency always to do things his own way rather than as instructed) and high marks academically. According to his fifth grade teacher, he was highly imaginative and inventive, and had an extremely sensitive and empathetic nature. He got along well with his classmates, but had few close friends outside of school. He won the science fair when he was in the sixth grade. There were many entries and details.

I found it odd that his parents started the log that far back. I could see them keeping any written reports from his school, but why start keeping a log of everything at such an early age, unless perhaps they did it retroactively when problems started surfacing; but, for what purpose?

On page six, when Todd was around age fourteen, they noted that he started becoming very obsessed with his grades and winning, wanting to always excel and be the best at everything. He became convinced that some of the methods he invented to win or excel were the key to any successes that he would or did achieve, rather any positive outcomes being due to his own nature or smarts. It was impossible to persuade him otherwise.

As I turned to the next page of the log, it suddenly occurred to me that our bedroom was at the front of the cabin, the side that faced the lake and away from the road leading up to the cabin. Todd might arrive back home and if he didn't call out to me as he came in, I might be none the wiser until he came bounding up the stairs and into the bedroom, seeing me, portfolio in hand.

I carried everything down the hallway and into the back room, which also had a sitting area in front of three large windows. From there, I would be able to see Todd drive up, giving me enough time to dash over to our bedroom and stash the portfolio underneath the bed once again. Other early warning tactics immediately sprang to mind behind that one. To give myself an extra edge in case I became too absorbed in the task of understanding more about the man I married and apparently, mistakenly thought I knew very well, I opened one of the windows a few inches to have an easier time hearing when Todd's car was approaching the cabin. I also adjusted the chair so that it faced the window more directly.

Satisfied and happy that I had relocated to the back bedroom, I settled into one of the chairs and continued from where I had left off.

There were examples of his success strategies—if they could be called that—throughout the next few pages. In one instance, Todd had received a perfect score on a math test including all the extra credit questions and attributed it to the fact that he was sitting next to his classmate, Paul. Paul, he believed, did not score as highly as him because Todd had reached those questions first on the test and had, through some force unbeknownst to him, siphoned the correct answers from Paul's head, leaving Paul unable to correctly respond to them. Todd felt guilty about it and tried to make amends, but there was no note about how he accomplished this, nor anything else related to the incident.

I sat there shaking my head. It was all so hard to believe. I wished his parents had included additional details about what happened. I wanted to know more. But, in his parent's defense, maybe they *didn't* know. I wondered how his parents learned about the incident though? From Todd? From his teachers? How else then? It seems odd that Todd would tell them. He never mentioned anything like it to me.

Thus far, there was not much detail related to any conversations between Todd and his parents, nor was there much information on what their own reactions to Todd's behavior were. I assume they were upset, or at least troubled, because they started keeping this log and wrote that 'it was impossible to persuade him otherwise'. From this, I inferred that they had tried to change Todd's way of thinking. But what did I know? For all I knew, they may have just inadvertently encouraged his bizarre fantasy world, helping it to grow.

The further I read, the more it seemed that whenever Todd lost at anything, it would affect him, sometimes making him moody and on occasion, terribly depressed, to the point he would lock himself in his room, refusing to come out and wanting to just be left alone. His mother had to leave his meals by the door. During these episodes, he would end up missing one or more days of school. He would then reemerge as if nothing had happened and be his cheerful old self again. This is when his parents first brought him to see a doctor. Besides this, the log made no mention of any other steps or actions taken by his parents thus far.

From time to time, I had brushed up against this moody side of his nature. He would become sullen and remote when returning from a visit with his family, especially if I asked him about how his trip went. I never pushed and just let it alone, not wanting to intrude. As a person, I have always considered myself approachable and sympathetic, and Todd talked to me, confided in me about many things, but never this. In retrospect, I can see that I probably should have pressed him more, gently pressed him, to talk about it.

A slamming car door caught my attention. Todd's car stopped just past the dirt road, at the edge of the large courtyard behind the cabin. An island of shrubbery partially hid the car, but I could see Todd starting to walk towards the cabin, shopping bag in hand. I ducked below the level of the windowsill and breathed a sigh of relief. He had brought me a simple gift.

I pulled the portfolio down onto the floor and stuffed the log back into it, then crouched-ran until out of sight of the window. Within seconds, I reached bedroom and shoved the portfolio back underneath our bed. I plopped myself down on the edge of the mattress and took a deep breath, as I tried to decide if I should head downstairs to greet him.

"I'm home, Bre." His voice sounded like it was coming from the living room.

I realized that I had left the window in the other room open.

"You upstairs?"

"Yes. I'm up here; just tidying up a bit." I wanted to go close it.

"Come down and see what I've got for you."

"Can't wait to see it. I'll be right down. Just give me a minute."

"You can finish tidying up later. C'mon. I want to show you my surprise," he said, growing impatient with my foot dragging. I could hear him coming up the stairs. My mind strayed, suddenly feeling insecure about whether I had pushed the portfolio far enough under the bed. I quickly double-checked that it wasn't visible, and smoothed out a ripple I saw on the bedspread.

Todd was standing in the doorway with an ear-to-ear smile. He held out the shopping bag. I got up and started to reach for it, but he pulled it back and swung it behind him, out of my reach.

"Kiss first," he said, his eyes beaming, as he patted his lips with the index finger of his free hand.

"If you don't want to give it to me, then don't." I walked over to mirror above the dresser and started fiddling with my hair. Todd followed.

"Not curious?"

"No," I said, playfully half-ignoring him.

"Not even a little bit curious?" Todd nonchalantly swung the shopping bag so that I could see it in the mirror.

I swung around, kissed him, and grabbed the bag out of his hand, which pleased him immensely, and ran over to the bed and pulled out the contents.

It was a beautiful, summery dress and some accessories to go with it—earrings, necklace, belt, and even some prettily designed pantyhose. I put the dress up against me and posed for Todd, then twirled around so that the flouncy skirt spun out as I did, continuing until I was directly in front of Todd.

"Thank you. It's beautiful," I said, a sigh of relief ricocheting back and forth through my high-pitched squeal of delight. "I totally love it."

"I knew you'd be pleased. It's my way of apologizing for revealing our community's story so abruptly last night. It's one of the harder parts of our ritual, but I'm so happy that you understand. I know it must have been quite a shock for you. But, you'll see. It'll work out and I'll be there to help you every step of the way."

Still holding the dress in front of me, I ran my hand over the skirt, pulled the waist into me, and turned to look at myself in the mirror.

"You stay here and put the dress on, then come downstairs. I have something else to show you. Just give me fifteen minutes before you come downstairs. Okay?"

"Bought me a pair of shoes to go with the dress, perhaps?"

I prayed that it was also something simple, some common, ordinary thing. But, as soon as I flung my guess at him, I realized that it couldn't be more clothing or accessories. Give him fifteen minutes. What could possibly take fifteen minutes?

Thinking I'd end up spoiling everything by playing twenty questions, I shut up about it, and instead, made a comical motion, in true slapstick fashion, as if I was going to race ahead of him to the stairs.

Todd grinned, winking one of his mischievously handsome brown eyes at me, and uttered a throaty, "nuh uh" admonishment, then turned on his heel, and headed down the stairs.

The dress fit perfectly. I put on the rest of his gift—the earrings, necklace, belt, and stockings. I put on some make-up, not too much—just a touch of color. I braided and re-braided my hair into a French twist, until my hair looked as perfect as the dress.

All of the sandals and shoes I had brought along looked horrible with the dress, completely detracting from the whole ensemble's light and airy aura. So, wanting to look as nice as possible in his gift, I decided to go barefoot and peeled off the stockings. Todd would probably scold me—as he usually did— for walking around without anything on my feet. If he wanted me to put my sandals on, I would, but *only* after I had a chance to show his gift off to him some more.

"Bre. Coming down?"

I glanced at the clock on the other side of the room. I had been so caught up making myself look as perfect as I could, primping and fussing, that over twenty-five minutes had gone by already.

"Be right there!" I said, as I looked myself over one last time in the mirror, and after re-straightening the dress's belt a bit, I was ready to make my grand entrance.

- 12 -

Todd was leaning against the wall at the foot of the stairs, anxiously waiting, his anxiety flowing out through the palms of his hands that were beating out a heavy, uneven rhythm against his thighs. As I came into view, and he became aware I was there, his hands stilled.

I paused at the top of the stairs—basking in Todd's wide-eyed admiration of his gift, of me in his gift. I had made him happy and I was glad.

He said nothing for a few more long moments. Then he extended his hand towards me, palm upturned, silently beckoning me to come down the stairs. My closed mouth curved into a modest smile and I slowly began walking down the stairs, not holding onto the banister, my arms down by my side.

The slight hesitations in my movements, from not holding onto the banister, seemed to delight him even more. But then, when I'd only four or five steps left to go, he could no longer contain himself and lunged toward my hand, hurrying me down the rest of the stairs and towards the kitchen, not stopping until we were in front of the basement door.

"The second part of my gift is downstairs, love."

"Downstairs?" I said, confused.

I removed my hand from his and rubbed my hands up and down against my upper arms, suddenly feeling a draft, in the warm and draft-less kitchen. Todd didn't comment at all about the sudden chill that had come over me nor did he chide me about my shoeless feet. His focus had completely shifted to part two of his gift and everything else fell out of sight and into its shadow.

"What is it?" I asked, reflexively, even though I knew it was probably silly and futile for me to do so.

Todd knit his brow, and his mouth twisted into a just have wait and see look that was tinged with a hopeful uncertainty of how I would react.

He flipped on the switch for the basement light, opened the door, and then motioned for me to go down the stairs ahead of him.

My husband, my husband that I adored, my husband that I loved with all my heart, was going to wear me out! I didn't know if I could keep up with the twists and turns of his illness.

Quite unlike the rest of the cabin, which was well adorned and immaculate, the narrow, poorly lit staircase leading down to the basement had no embellishments or decorations of any kind. The unfinished plywood stairs felt scratchy beneath my feet, and from what I could tell, it seemed like the steps had been rather hastily painted over.

"The stairs are kind of rough. Maybe I should go get my sandals," I said, turning around. I never thought I'd hear myself saying that. But, under the circumstances, I was a bit leery of going down the basement barefoot. "Be right back."

Todd didn't move aside to let me go by him.

"Hey! You're the one that's always on me about walking around without my shoes."

"Sure. Sure. Alright," he said. He was kind of annoyed, but made room for me to pass by.

When I returned a few minutes later, I found Todd sitting on a kitchen chair, leaning forward. He looked up at me, his eagerness gone, something obviously troubling him, and I felt like my interruption had put a damper on his enthusiasm.

"I'm back. Let's go." Todd got up and followed me over to the basement door. "I'm dying to see what it is!" I said, doing my best to pump some excitement back into him. He gave me a kiss, then moved away and started drumming his fingers on the nearby counter.

"Maybe we should just forget about the gift for now," he said, somewhat dejected. "You look so pretty in your new dress."

"Thank you," I said, growing more concerned about his state of mind by the moment.

"Let's drive over to Newton and walk around a bit," he continued. "It's getting too late for antiquing, but we'd still have time to browse through one or two shops today. Afterwards, we can find a nice restaurant to have dinner at."

Feeling bad for having taken the wind out of his sails, I said, "I want to see your gift first. C'mon. I'm sure I'll love it. You know you want to show it to me." Todd stopped drumming, but stayed over by the counter, not looking at me.

"Please."

"Okay," he said, his ambivalence receding.

I started down the stairs once again and Todd followed close behind, shutting the door behind him. I lost my footing somewhat as the door closed and the additional light from the kitchen vanished. Todd caught my arm and steadied me until I had regained my balance.

"Leave the door open. It'll cast more light on the stairs," I blurted, to which he replied, apologetically, "It has to stay shut. You'll be fine. Just go slow."

Halfway down the stairs, I got a whiff of an odd scent, which mingled with and then dissipated into the unpleasant, stale musty odor of the basement. The stairs needed sweeping; the shadowy edges of the steps had piles dust on them, sharply contrasting the cleaner middle area. I didn't know how often the steps had been used, but it must have been often enough to prevent a lot of dust from settling in the middle.

A rough veneer of concrete covered the walls. Affixed high up, on the left wall, was a light encased in a dark gold glass shade. It cast just enough light to make the steps visible. Expensive furniture upstairs and can't afford better lighting for the basement stairs! But, who knows what their reasons were. Maybe they were the type that only spent money where it shows.

There was no handrail, so I steadied myself by pressing my palms against the damp wall on either side.

I did not like the creepy staircase one bit. Having second thoughts yet again, I suggested, "Why don't you just bring whatever it is you want to give me upstairs?"

"I can't. You need to come downstairs to see it. I know it's kind of dreary; sorry about that. There's another light a little bit further on in the basement. You have to feel along the wall for the switch."

When I reached the bottom of the stairs, Todd put his hand on my shoulder, holding me from moving forward.

"Hang on. Wait right here. I'll turn on the other light." I stepped aside so that Todd could pass by me.

The basement was dark except for a meager amount of hazy striped light coming through a small, thick, opaque window on the opposite side. After walking several yards away, the darkness swallowed him and I could only see a vague shadow moving near the wall. I was grateful that he kept talking as he hunted for the light switch.

Todd flipped on the light.

I screamed and my legs collapsed underneath me, causing my back hit the wall hard before I slid down and landed on the edge of the bottom step, and then bounced off it onto the floor.

- 13 -

Todd rushed over to me. He was speaking, but I couldn't hear what he was saying. The pulsing in my ears was drowning him out. My whole body was pulsating, as silent tears ran uncontrollably down my cheeks.

He knelt down beside me and took me in his arms, pressing my head against his chest, my head facing away from the interior of the basement and the sight I couldn't bear to look at. Slowly, my hearing returned.

"I'm sorry. Please forgive me, Bre. I knew it would be hard for you. It's not easy for me either."

On a mat, in a far corner of the basement, shackled to the wall, was the woman I had seen at the restaurant yesterday. And she was unconscious.

Todd loosened his hold and settled himself down on the floor next to me, resting his back against the wall. I couldn't bring myself to look up yet.

"She's my gift to you."

'What?' I thought. *'What did you just say? I don't think I heard you right'.* When he referred to her as his 'gift' to me, I was poised to interrupt him. I was glad I didn't.

Todd shifted his position slightly and put his arm back around me. "It wasn't easy getting her here," he said. "She hates me. She didn't tell me in so many words, but I know she does ... She never could understand how things are, Bre. She has utterly forsaken me. You understand though."

But, I didn't understand. I didn't understand at all! I knew that Todd would think it odd if I said nothing in return, but what could I say. The seconds were flying by, each one ticking more forcefully than the last. My husband was sick. I knew that. I loved him in spite of his illness, and still wanted to help him. My husband did not have a violent tendency or a mean bone in his body.

Yet, there she was—kidnapped and shackled to the wall. I buried my head against Todd's arm, trying to calm down before I said something impulsively that I'd be sure to regret and struggled hard to suppress the overwhelming urge I had to deny what was happening.

The only thing I knew right now was that this needed to end before something worse happened. And it was starting to sink into my thick skull that this was really too much for me to handle.

"You rest a few minutes; we have time," Todd said, gently wiping my tears away, and then lowering his head so that it was resting on top of mine. And we stayed this way for many long minutes.

Todd was much sicker than his parents had led me to believe. But, maybe they didn't know, just as I hadn't known or even suspected during the whole time we were dating. I didn't expect his family, well intentioned or not, would be much help. They'd only make things worse.

Over and over again, the words 'she was my gift' swirled around my brain. The only implications I could draw from it were ones my mind refused to accept. Finally, I concluded that the only thing I could do at this point was to stall as much as possible and play along with him until I saw an opportunity to act and help us all get away from the influence of Todd's fantasy world.

Clinging tightly to Todd and gathering my courage, I opened my eyes and looked out into the basement. She was still there; unmoving; slumped over; shackles around her neck and all four of her limbs, pinning her to the wall with short stretches of sturdy looking chains, a cloth coiled loosely around the neck shackle.

"What's her name?" I asked. His parents had told me her name—Janie—last night, but since Todd wasn't aware of this, I needed to obtain some of the same information from him and mind my Ps and Qs, being careful not to mention something I was not supposed to know.

In a low voice, he spat out her name. "Jane."

I had hoped he'd volunteer some clues as to what he expected, but he said nothing else.

I was going to try to show some interest and ask 'How'd you manage to bring her here?' but I didn't want to encourage him any further. Still, I felt like I had to acknowledge the situation somehow, and what he had done.

"You went to a lot of trouble for me," I said.

He pulled me closer and kissed the side of my forehead, but still, maddeningly, said nothing further about her or the situation.

Suddenly, I was stricken with the notion that she might not actually be unconscious, that my assumption might have been wrong. I had to check on her.

"I'd like to take a closer look at her," I said, then slowly got up, my legs still shaky, and looked at Todd, waiting for some acknowledgement. He brightened at my non-judgmental display of interest.

There were no obvious indications that a violent physical struggle of any kind had taken place. She had no cuts or bruising that I could see. And she was still breathing—thank goodness. But every time she inhaled, I could hear a raspy sound as if she was having difficulty breathing.

I tried to press my thoughts into her brain, thinking as forcefully as I could muster, 'Don't stop breathing, Janie. Please don't stop breathing'.

"Her breathing sounds funny to me."

"She has a touch of asthma. That's all."

I looked over at Todd and said, trying not to sound too panicky, "Doesn't she need her inhaler or something then?"

"No. Her asthma's not that bad. Anyway, she'll be okay for the ceremony," Todd said, puzzled as to why I was so concerned—why I was asking such an irrelevant question.

I jostled her shoulder, but she remained unconscious. I wondered if he had drugged her, made her breathe in something that had made her go unconscious, and was now affecting her breathing.

This area of the basement didn't appear to be used for much. It was unfinished and sparsely furnished. There were a couple of tall stand-alone closets, an old-fashioned sink, and a small table with two chairs. Piled on the table were the items that Todd had brought down from the kitchen the day before to store in the extra refrigerator, which I didn't see anywhere.

The middle of the cement floor had a drain around which white streaks radiated out in all directions, apparent remnants of something that had been poured down the drain and not completely cleaned up. There was also a door near to where Janie was lying which I guessed led to another part of the basement. From its proximity, it didn't look like it would open up to any cellar steps leading to the outside of the cabin, but more likely into another room—perhaps the boiler room or where the second refrigerator might be.

I went over to the table and starting casually shifting around some of the items and picked one of them out. I turned around, holding a package of cheese in my outstretched hand. Todd didn't look over at me. He didn't notice. His eyes were fixated on Janie.

"Hungry?" I said, upset by the sight of the food, but trying to speak in as non-sarcastic a voice as I could muster.   It was especially disconcerting because this particular lie seemed to have been of a more deliberate variety; one that could not be excused or explained away by his illness.

Barely acknowledging me and not at all ruffled or concerned by my discovery, he replied, "They *used* to have an extra frig. Guess they got rid of it or something," and after a brief look in my direction, he went right back to staring at Janie.

I bit my tongue, and then I bit it again and put the cheese back down on the table.   We had arguments like any other couple, although they were an infrequent occurrence, but nothing that had occurred between us before this 'refrigerator incident' had ever made me so upset. I had never felt lied to before and I was now more confused than ever. Why didn't he tell me about it yesterday when he came back up from the basement, after having found the refrigerator gone? He told me he transferred the extra food to the second refrigerator that was down there.

In hearing all the revelations over the past two days, I had felt concerned, worried, sad, hopeful, and scared at times, but never angry, never deliberately lied to. I had felt he couldn't help the lies he told or was afraid to tell the truth, perhaps. This just didn't seem to fit that pattern.

But, what did I know about anything. Apparently nothing it seemed. And I felt guilty for being angry because it probably really was an aspect of his illness. It had to be.

I remained sitting on a chair near the table for maybe ten or fifteen minutes, silently looking at Todd as he sat, motionless, staring at Janie, oblivious to me, oblivious to his surroundings.

I thought about my cell phone upstairs in the bedroom.

"Todd—"

Not even a quick glance in my direction this time.

I got up, walked over to the basement stairs, and started up them. Halfway up I turned around to see if Todd had noticed. He hadn't. Reaching the top step, I turned the knob on the basement door and pushed.

It didn't open. I released the knob, then tried again, this time using more force, but still had no success in opening it. Had Todd locked the door behind us without my noticing it? I found that hard to believe. I would have heard him doing so. But, what other explanation could there be?

I came back down the stairs.

"The door's locked," Todd matter-of-factly said as I passed by him. He hadn't been as oblivious as he had seemed.

"I need to go to the bathroom."

Now I had Todd's attention.   After wrestling
with himself, he offered, "Yea, me too.   I'll come
upstairs with you," and as he stood up, I managed a
weak, close-mouthed smile in response.

"Why'd you lock the door?"

"What's gotten into you, Bre?   What a silly
question to ask," he said, shaking his head at me,
disappointed.   Then after reconsidering, he added,
"You're kind of tired, huh?"

"I *am* a bit tired.   I guess I haven't totally
recuperated from all the wedding stuff."

Todd unlocked the door.   He left both lights
on—the stairway light and the one in the basement.
That was a relief. I didn't want poor Janie to regain
consciousness and wake up in darkness—not that
waking up in shackles wouldn't be horrible enough.

"Why don't you use the bathroom down here
and I'll go upstairs and use the one up there," I said,
taking a few steps towards the living room before
Todd jumped in front of me.

"No. I'll use the upstairs bathroom. I want to get some things from the cabinet underneath the sink for later—"

Ripples of confusion washed over my face.

"—for your and Jane's ceremony," he added, his voice betraying his growing impatience with my slow-wittedness. Last night's offer to help me understand was starting to become an annoying encumbrance and he was growing weary of having to explain every little thing to me.

I wanted to see what he was going upstairs to get. I needed to know, even though a part of me didn't want to know.

"Then we'll both go upstairs. I want to change my clothes, anyway. I've gotten dirt all over the beautiful dress you gave me," I said, gently brushing the smudges with the back of my hand. "Sorry about that. I should change out of it before I get it any more messed up. I can bring it to the cleaners when we get back home."

His face transformed into an inscrutable deep ocean, and my pent-up nervousness broke loose and overpowered me.

"Thank you again for the dress," I said, kissing him on the lips. He didn't kiss me back. Ignoring that, I excitedly continued, "It really was so thoughtful of you to get it for me. Next week—"

"You think I'm stupid?" Todd interjected flatly, his eyes narrowing.

"What? Of course not. *What are you talking about?*"

"You don't *really* understand. *Do you*, Bre?"

"Don't understand. Don't understand what?"

"You're just humoring me. You've probably been humoring me all along."

"What? What are you saying? I love you. Why would I do that? I wouldn't do that."

"You're worse than Jane. At least she was honest," he said, with hostility, and grabbing my arm, he gruffly began dragging me back towards the basement door, his fingers digging deep into my flesh. "She was the first girl I ever truly loved. We could have been so happy together if only she'd have understood how things are and accepted them. But, she couldn't. She just couldn't understand."

Hope drained from me, splashing loudly around my feet. In shock, I let myself be dragged. But, when we got to the doorway, a vision of being pushed down the stairs assaulted and blinded me. I smashed into him and yanked myself away from him, twisting and turning and clawing, trying to escape his grasp—but I couldn't; he was too strong and I relented.

"Todd! What's gotten into you? Please. You're hurting me. Think about what you're doing. I love you. I love you. You know I love you. I don't understand why you're doing this. I know you love me too. I know you do. Please stop. Things will work out."

I threw words at him. I wasn't his wife any more. I wasn't human. I was just a mindless mass of fear, hurling futile word after word at him— hoping one of the words would hook on.

He pushed me onto the stairs and against the wall, and then with a soul-crushing, disdainful scowl on his face, he pulled me away from the wall and slammed me back against the wall, hard—hard enough to push the air out of my lungs—as if warning me not to move, to stay put.

He stood there for a few moments, glaring his disappointment at me. I fell mute. Words were pointless.

Then he was gone.

And I was locked in.

- 14 -

Despair enveloped me. For a long time, I just sat on the top step, with my body and hands pressed up against the door, floating near the edges of a lifeless vacuum.

I could hear him moving about. He was still in the kitchen.

I thought of the happy times we had shared. I thought of all our plans for a bright future together—of children, of our own home, of shared memories, of growing together, of enduring love. They were a fantasy—my own.

There was Todd, proud papa, snapping a picture of our little Kathleen as she took her first steps. There we were, having a picnic with our four children. It was a gorgeous, sunny, country day. The kids were playing badminton on the grass without a net. There we all were, driving across the country in our brand new station wagon, singing, the kids making up stories about the people in the cars that we passed.

The sounds came and went. Todd went into another room, and then came back again. The outside kitchen door opened and shut, opened and shut. Boxes were set down. Metal clanked. A pot? No. The sound was higher pitched.

The stairway light turned off. Only a seam of light shined from underneath the door. I held my breath. The basement light remained on.

Silence.

My strength had deserted me. Thoughts of finding a way to sneak out of the cabin crashed up against me, washed over my face, and then ebbed away, merging with rivulets of free flowing slow tears.

Odd sounds came from the other side of the door. The other side of the door was far away. Another country. Another language I did not understand.

A faint "Uuuuhhhhhh" drifted up from the basement.

Janie was regaining consciousness, poking holes in my shroud of despair.

"Get a grip, Bridget!" I commanded. "Snap out of it."

———

She was very groggy, not fully conscious yet.

I jostled her, imploring her to "Wake up, Janie. C'mon wake up." I shook her a bit harder.

With half-close eyes, she managed to utter a raspy trying-hard-to-wakeup noise and then raised one of her hands to her temple, rubbing it. In her semi-conscious state, the shackle was too heavy for her arm, and after a few moments, her hand slid down to her shoulder under the weight of it.

Janie's eyes widened as she suddenly became aware of the shackle around her neck, and then the other metal restraints on her arms and legs. She began backing away from me, trying to put as much distance between us as her chains allowed.

Afraid that she was going to start screaming and cause Todd to become more upset and come downstairs, I motioned for her to stay calm and tried as best as I could—being in unsure territory myself—to allay her fears. "It's okay, Janie. I'm not going to hurt you. I'm trapped down here too."

She started wheezing and then grabbed at one of the shackles, trying to squeeze her hand out of it, but it was too tight.

"Shhh. Shhh. Calm down. You'll make your wheezing worse."

She looked at me; confused; not trusting; not fully awake.

"How do you know ... my name?" Who are you?" She stopped to catch her breath, exhausted already.

"I'm Todd's wife, his second wife."

"Where's Todd? ... He kidnapped me," she said, calmer now, and tried, with her diminished strength, to squeeze her hand through the shackle one more time.

"He's upstairs I think. He's locked me down here with you. He's terribly upset. I don't know when he's coming back down, but he's locked the basement door.

"Did you see anything, Janie?" I said, moving over to the door by Janie and turning the knob. It was locked. "Do you know what he did with the key to your shackles?"

Janie moved her head slightly from side to side.

"Do you have a cell phone on you? Anything we can use?"

Janie moved her head from side to side once more.

"Todd told me you have a touch of asthma. Maybe if you rest your back against the wall, kind of half sitting, half lying down, it will help your asthma some, help you breathe a little easier."

She pulled at the cloth surrounding the neck iron. Todd had probably put the cloth there to help cushion her neck, but it now seemed to be worsening her breathing difficulties. It had bunched up on one side.   I adjusted the cloth to create more space between it and her neck.   I thought it best not to remove it entirely.

"I wish there was something better for you to rest against." Her breathing still sounded bad to me, but I didn't want to say it and alarm her further.

"I don't have asthma … I think he must have drugged me.   My head's pounding … I don't feel well."   I helped her re-position herself against the wall, half sitting up, and her breathing improved a bit.

"Maybe there's something in one of those closets over there that we can use," I said, getting up and walking over to them.   She remained resting by the opposite wall.

Helping Janie was helping me; helping me stay calm; helping me not think about my blighted future; and I was grateful not to be alone.   I didn't want to leave her here alone either though.

I pulled on the handle of the first closet.   It didn't open.   I yanked it harder and the not-too-sturdy closet swayed a bit.   My free hand immediately swung up to steady it. A couple of the items that were inside thudded on the metal shelves and it sounded like something broke. I didn't want to risk toppling the closet over, so I stopped trying to pull it open. There was nothing around to try prying it open with. The other cabinet was locked also.

A slight stomach-turning odor began emanating from the first closet, merging with the vague, unrecognizable odor that was already lingering in the air. I retreated to the other side of the basement.

"I can't get either of the closets open."

"Don't worry about it. I'm still so ... woozy though. I wish ... I wish I could be of more help."

I tried squeezing her hands through the shackles, but had no more luck with that than Janie did. The chains looked solidly bolted to the wall and didn't look like they'd budge. I had to try them though. I wrapped one of her arm chains around my hand and pulled against the wall bolt in short bursts, but hard as I tried, I wasn't able to dislodge it.

I gave the chain attached to her other arm a try. Same result. Even putting my foot against the wall for leverage didn't have any effect. Looking at my sandal clad feet, I was glad I had gone back upstairs to put them on.

"How are we going to get out of here?" Janie asked.

"I don't know. ... I don't know," I said, glancing around the room. Finding a way out of this awful situation didn't look too promising. "We'll think of something."

I cared about Todd, but his illness aside, he was not thinking clearly and I felt like he had now veered even further into his fantasy world. Janie and I needed to get to some place safe. Once we were safe, we could get help for Todd. I never dreamed he could be capable of this. I felt bad that in trying to help him, in trying to figure out how best to help, I had said something—done something—to set him off. I had no clue what he'd do or how to put things right.

Whenever I closed my eyes, an image appeared of the terrible scowl he had on his face when he last looked at me. But, as the minutes passed, I felt less sad, less scared, and more resolved. Things would work out.

"There's a sink over there. Do you want some water, Janie?"

"Thank you, yes," she said, smiling weakly.

I turned the handle for the cold water and studied the water flowing out from the faucet. From what I could tell, it appeared to be all right, so I stuck my head under, and took a tentative sip. It tasted okay, but I only took a few more sips, not wanting to drink too much under the circumstances even though I was feeling somewhat thirsty.

Cupping my hands, I filled them with water, and kept them tightly together as I gingerly walked back over to Janie, leaving the faucet running. I moved my hands up to her lips, but she could only take one sip before turning her head away. The remainder fell to the floor on my way back to the sink to shut the water back off.

We seemed stuck here. The only other door, the one next to where Janie was resting, was locked also, and the only basement window was barred.

"He came to see me this afternoon," Janie said.
"... I told him to stay away from me. We argued
and the next thing I remember is waking up here ...
Where are we?"

"We're at his aunt and uncle's cabin by the lake.
Has Todd ever taken you here?" I asked, in hopes
she might know the cabin well enough to think of
something that could help us. I began eyeing the
door near Janie again, looking for the hinges. They
were on other side.

"He did take us here once ... on our
honeymoon." Her eyes were starting to droop again.
"The basement looks different than I remember it
though. Emptier ... It was terrible. Terrible ... He
wanted me to participate in some kind of ritual. He
left the basement door open though. I managed to
knock him unconscious when he was distracted and
ran away ... but even though I tried to talk with him
after our divorce, make things better between us ...
try get him to move on with his life, he won't leave
me be ... I'm sorry ... I'm feeling kind of drowsy ...
Maybe we can talk more—"

Her voice trailed off.

I shook my head. This whole ordeal was just too horrifying to be real. Staring at her chains, I was still finding it hard to believe Todd could do such a thing.

"I don't understand how Todd could do this. He's always had such a gentle nature."

Her brows knit in confusion just before she passed out. I shook her but she was out cold again.

I sat down on the mat next to her and lifted one of her hands to have a closer look at the shackle, hoping to find a way to free her hand. It was an inch wide and about a quarter of an inch thick with a flat, highly polished surface. I had assumed that they were like what I had always imagined shackles to be—that is, having a lock—but when I inspected the surface, it was completely smooth except for four vertical seams. No lock was visible and the attached chain appeared to be welded on. The side had a number of layers made from some kind of steel-looking material.

I pulled, twisted, pried, pushed, and tried manipulating it every which way. Finally, after five minutes or so, one of the seams opened and I was able to remove her hand. However, I didn't know— didn't remember—exactly what maneuver had done the trick, and inspecting the open ends didn't provide any clues. With Janie's hand now free, I tried to get it to lock again, but couldn't.

Picking up Janie's other hand, I set about twisting and turning the shackle, but after about ten minutes of this, the shackle was still firmly in place, and I thought, perhaps, I'd have better luck with one of the other shackles and the trick to opening the lock would become more apparent.

If I could do it once, I could do it again. It seemed odd though that Todd would use this type of shackle to restrain her. If a person could eventually get out of it, what was the point? Perhaps, he didn't expect Janie to try anything other than what she had before—squeezing her hand through the opening. But still, the question lingered.

The basement door opened and the light from the kitchen became visible.

- 15 -

Todd did not appear in the doorway.

I stayed put. Waiting.

Still, no Todd.

I debated whether to go up the stairs. It would be terrible for Janie to regain consciousness once more and find me gone. But, what choice was there?

Minutes passed.

Still, no Todd.

I began cautiously climbing the stairs, my ears straining to pick up the slightest sound. I got about halfway up the stairs when Todd suddenly pealed himself away from the wall and appeared in the doorway. The sudden, unexpected appearance of him smashed into me and I stopped abruptly, remaining frozen against the wall. Only my heart was moving, pounding against my ribcage, at first from the initial shock of seeing him suddenly appear, and then from the rising sense of dread, not knowing what the next few moments would bring.

Todd lifted his hand and extended his arm towards me—his face, melting into the softness of forgiveness.

"I forgive you, Bre. I hope you can forgive me too. I know you would never do what I accused you of before. Come," he said, motioning for me to come the rest of the way up the stairs.

As I neared the top step, he clasped my hand in his and walked us over to the kitchen table. Much to my chagrin, my disobedient hand started shaking uncontrollably. Todd could feel the tremor and the undercurrent of alarm running through me, and he took both of my hands in his, a habit that had always given me a feeling being safe—cared for.

"I'm sorry," he continued, as I looked at him, searching for answers. "I know I threw quite a scare into you. I shouldn't have said those things I did to you about Janie—shouldn't have compared you to her. You know I love you, Bre. You've given me so much strength, so much happiness. I don't ever want to be without you."

"I do forgive you," I said. "We'll put it past us and forget about it." It wasn't a lie. I did forgive him. How could I not?

What my friend Nancy always used to say ran through my mind once again, 'the only way out is through'. I couldn't leave Janie down there with Todd in the condition he was in and I wasn't in any position to call for help either, not without running the risk of Todd finding out before any help arrived, and I shuttered to think what direction he'd spiral off into if he caught me. Somehow, I had to convince Todd that he needed to seek professional help—had to make him come to that conclusion himself.

Todd had regained his patience and he was doing his best to maintain his composure and not succumb completely to the dictates of his ever-evolving fantasy world. He was trying. He really was. And for that, I was grateful.

The kitchen looked the same as it had before, as least as far I could recall. There were no remnants, no traces at all of his recent comings and goings, except an ominous bottle of wine and two already poured glasses next to it on the table. Hard as I tried to focus on Todd, they kept pulling my attention in their direction.

"I took it for granted that you understood more than you really did ... do, but I can see that you're at least trying to understand my world, my culture. I'm so sorry I was short with you before. I didn't mean to scare you. I guess I'm just so impatient for you to know everything, and truly become part of our community. I don't want there to be any secrets."

I slipped my hands out from between his, as gently and unobtrusively as I could manage—the shaking had subsided, but was still there—and touched my hand to Todd's cheek, my face a reflection of my desire to really understand him and the world he inhabited.

But, a momentary lapse in focus and the gravitational force of the wine glasses pulled my eyes over towards them, holding mercilessly onto my gaze.

"It's a little something to drink a toast to us with … to put our little quarrel behind us."

Todd picked up the glasses and extended one of them in my direction, silently compelling me to take it from his hand.

"To a long and happy future together," he said. But when he motioned for us to drink, I hesitated.

"I know you're not partial to wine, but it's really quite good. It's a very mild wine—practically tastes like grape juice, your favorite. I think you'll like this one."

I hesitated still.

He began again. "To getting back on the right course," he said, tapping my glass with his own.

I looked at the glass, still not taking a sip.

Todd urged me on. "Go ahead," he said.

Todd took a sip.

I complied, barely taking a sip. It tasted okay— nothing peculiar.

Then he downed the rest. A few gulps and his wine glass was empty.

"Bottoms up, Bre" he said, eager for me to do likewise.

Todd watched as my hand drifted over to the table and I set the glass down near the wine bottle, a good ways in from the edge of the table, putting a damper on his celebratory mood. I turned away from him and plopped my elbows on the table, resting my chin on my hands, and looked out the back window, trying to think how I could convince Todd to seek help. I prayed that my one little sip was sufficient and that he'd let the toast idea go.

"It must be so difficult, especially since you're obligated never to tell very many people about your practices and—"

"C'mon, Bre," he cajoled, lifting my glass and tapping it against my hand that was closest to him. "Don't you want to toast to our future."

He wasn't going to let it drop.

"Hey. I took a sip. In my book that counts as a full-fledged toast," I said, and mustering a stern schoolmarm smile, I added, "Got it, buddy!"

"Alright! Alright! I give up little miss technicality. Geez! I never met anyone who disliked wine so much as you," he said, wrapping his arms around me and giving me a big squeeze, distracting me even further from my mission.

Todd wanted to toast about us getting back on the right course. An image of poor Janie, down in the basement, popped into my head, making me change *my* course. Nudging him away, I started down another please-let-this-be-the right-path once again. "You said last night that you'd help me—help me to understand. You said to ask you any questions I had. Did you really mean that?"

"Of course I did. I said I was sorry for being—"

"Don't you see? I'm afraid to ask you about things."

"But, why? Why would you be afraid? You can ask me anything—anything at all," Todd said, concerned and saddened that his recent behavior may have left me feeling this way. "Please. What is it you want to know?"

"You'll think 'Oh, my goodness! What a stupid girl I married', stupid for asking such ridiculous questions and for being so obtuse."

"I won't. I swear. I *want* you to ask me questions. I'm sorry if I made you feel that way. I'm happy you're taking an interest. Really I am. Please … ask away."

"You'll maybe think me ungrateful."

Todd sat back in his chair, struggling to process the unfathomable bombshell I had just thrown at him, unable to figure out what I could possibly be ungrateful about.

"I don't like my gift," I blurted out. Todd froze. Not the reaction I had expected, but I ignored it and pressed on, trying to shake him into giving me what I wanted and hardly pausing to take a breath. "I don't understand what she's doing here and what's more, her being here is very upsetting. What I really want is for her to leave, for you to take off her shackles, and tell her to go home. Then what I want is for you to leave her be. Permanently."

He was listening intently. I decided to risk jarring him a bit further, banking on his desire to please and make me happy, in hopes of getting him to release Janie. So, as much as I hated saying it and possibly hurting him, I flung at him, "I think you still love her. That's what I think!"

Todd was dumbfounded. His jaw dropped and he just sat there staring at me.

Second after second went by without any response from Todd, prompting me to have second thoughts about the approach I took. Todd looked down at his shoes and I could see him wrestling with a thought that was quickly chewing him up, and me along with him.

I thought 'Oh my God. What did I do?'

I wanted to get Janie to safety and not have to worry about her well-being on top of worrying about my own situation and Todd's unpredictability. Her situation had seemed so much more of a priority. I thought if I sounded stern and upset, without being judgmental about him kidnapping her and locking her up down the basement, it would prod Todd into releasing Janie, if only just to make me happy.

He looked up at me, completely crestfallen. Not the reaction I had hoped to elicit. My mind raced, trying to recover.

"You see. I told you," I said. "Dumb. Dumb. Dumb. Now you're mad at me."

"If you really want me to, I'll take her back home, but, later. I can't take her back home now."

"I don't see why she can't just leave now. You don't need to drive her. She can go by herself." When he didn't respond, I suggested, "Just let her walk home or she can take the bus or a taxi."

"I don't want to lose you, Bre," Todd replied, looking at his feet, not at me, unable to bring himself to look at my face for fear of what he'd see there. The same sudden feeling of sadness descended upon him that I had seen previously when he returned home from visiting with his family and I had asked him about his trip. It was a mistake, pushing so hard.

"I'm here for good," I said, firmly grasping his arm and shaking it. "You're stuck with me." His eyes ventured up and I smiled, trying to latch on, but his mind had drifted too far away and he could not be cheered up.

He just quietly replied, "Would you mind very much if we continued our conversation about this later? I'll answer whatever questions you have."

"Sure. Sure. We can do it later ... everything will work out. I know it will. A year from now, we'll be all settled into our new life together."

But, actually, I really didn't know anymore if we would have a life together—if we *could* have a future together. As much as I loved Todd, I didn't know anymore.

Todd shook his head in agreement, but he was only half-listening, and I don't think he believed me. He headed into the living room area, drained, his usually agile gait replaced by the walk of someone who was very weary—mentally weary.

I called after him, wanting to make him feel better, "Wait—"

He turned around, waiting. I could see that he felt he had yet again disappointed. But, no words came to me. All I could do was to offer a sympathetic smile and he turned back around and left.

I didn't know what else to do to reach him or help any of us and I felt bad that I had caused him pain. This was not going well at all.

After a while, I peeked into the living room. Todd was slouched on the sofa, one leg up, one down, and the television was turned on to some news show where a group of financial analysts were having a heated discussion.

"Todd—" I tested, calling out to him, not shouting, but loud enough so that he should have been able to hear me above the animated banter coming from the television screen. I tried one more time, a little louder.

He didn't hear me and so I headed upstairs and into our bedroom, then fished my phone out from the bottom of my handbag and unlocked it.

- 16 -

Suddenly, someone was suffocating me.   A hand was pressing a cloth tightly over my mouth and nose, another was pinning my arms down by my side. I gasped, sucking part of the cloth in and out of my mouth with each breath, as the noxious fumes raced passed my coughing and down into my lungs.

I struggled to free myself, looking down at the blanched knuckles of the offending hand, at the familiar scar across Todd's index finger, at his wedding ring. Then my cell phone dropped from my hand into the blurry void.

I dreamed—weird, terrible dreams. I was back in the basement again and I was lying on a cold metal table. There were straps around my wrists and ankles holding me down onto the table. My head throbbed and I couldn't see very well through the blue haze.

Janie started screaming in the distance, weakly shouting volumes of pleas, insults, and threats at someone—someone behind me. Bits of her words sprayed onto my face as they shot past me and then quickly evaporated, only a few words lingering long enough to seep in. Shouts of "sick ... do whatever ... tell me what ... assist you ... please just let me go." Her words seeped in as the pounding inside my skull slammed against them. Then Janie stopped, and there was only the throbbing of my head against the peaceful quiet.

A needle slid into my arm and the pounding faded. Happiness enveloped me. The blue haze glided away and I saw Todd standing over me. He leaned over my body and stroked my cheek with the palm side of his hand.

"Rest, darling. My family will be here soon."

His voice was far away. I was warm and happy. I closed my eyes and drifted off into a sea of sweet memories—going roller-skating with my childhood friends, my mother's cool hand on my fever-drenched forehead, the marvel of an abstract sculpture my art class created, walking down the aisle at my wedding and the sight of Todd waiting for me at the altar. The world was fuzzy and beautiful ... and I drifted.

Then awareness of where I was crashed into me, stark and cold, and I awakened into a state of shocked confusion. My eyes frantically darted around the room, voraciously sucking everything in. First, over to Todd, who was standing over me, his eyes filled with love. In his hand, a needle with the plunger pushed all the way in. Then, over to Janie, slumped over, her hair matted with blood. Then over to the no-longer-barred window and the rays of daylight streaking through it—had I been laying here all night? Then, over to the camera whose light was making my eyes tear, the blood on Todd's sleeve, the metal table underneath me, my restraints, the small table upon which an empty basin rested.

I screamed against the duct tape covering my mouth, snorting chunks of air into my nose, and battling the restraints on my arms and legs, making myself light-headed in the process.

Todd put a gentle, strong hand on my shoulder and my thrashing ceased at his hand's command, my eyes fixating on his.

"Shhh, my darling. Everything's okay," he said, caressing my shoulder, and trying to comfort me. "I love you so much. I never want to be without you."

I screeched through the duct tape, "Oh my God, Todd. What is this? What are you doing?" but all that emerged was a muffled, unintelligible garble.

"Shhh. Shhh. I'll explain everything to you ... and I'll be with you every step of the way. I can hardly wait, Bre."

Todd covered my face with kisses, and in my panic, I banged into his head with my own. He jumped back, startled, his eyes lighting up, overcome by my enthusiasm.

"You're anxious too, my love. I know. It is a bit scary though. But, also exciting at the same time, no? I have so much hope for us. I can't tell you how much, Bre." Todd's hold on reality had completely crumbled, his fantasy world now had full reign over him. Any vestiges of my husband, my Todd, were gone.

And as the tears streamed down my face, Todd continued, pointing to the camera, mounted on a tripod near the foot of the table.

"My parents, my aunt and uncle, and Jack are upstairs in the living room waiting for me to give them the signal to turn on the television. I wanted them to be here on this happy occasion—to share it with us. I have the strength I need now, thanks to you. I've figured out a way to do what I must do— am supposed to do—and until now, could not."

Todd turned away from me and continued, "I'm sad to tell you that my family witnessed my previous aborted attempts on many an occasion."

And Janie must have been one of those attempts. Janie, who ran away from him on their honeymoon, but not far enough.

"I've tried hard, so hard, but as I confessed to you this morning, I can't seem to awaken the cannibal instinct in myself. All my attempts at becoming a true cannibal, someone my culture could be proud of, have been horrible failures.

"Whatever strength and talents I've managed to absorb from others have been fleeting, nothing, impermanent ... always needing to be replenished. And it's been so exhausting. But, I no longer need to do that."

Todd turned back around, and bending forward, he gazed into my eyes, as he reached for my hand, clasping it in his.

"With you, my job, my new promotion will seem a mere cakewalk. No telling what great things we can achieve—together! I'm so lucky to have found you."

Todd noticed me squeezing my wrist against the top edge of the other arm restraint, a concerned furrow forming on his brow.

"I'm sorry. I know the restraints are a little bit uncomfortable. I'll take them off you soon," he said, disappearing into the back part of the basement, behind my head. I could hear him unlocking the metal cabinet that I had tried unsuccessfully to unlock, and taking items off the shelves. Then Todd hurriedly wheeled what sounded like the serving cart over in my direction, positioning it at the head of the table, and began organizing the items he had removed from the cabinet.

Then a rush of air, and shifting shadows, as he unfurled and shook open a robe and put it on. Cologne wafted through the air. Todd never wore cologne. A click and relaxing, soft romantic instrumental music began encircling my head, then moved closer, further muffling any other sounds. A wisp of a kiss as he reappeared, wearing a black robe decorated with nausea-inducing broad red swirls of color near the edges.

Tears streamed as I prayed that things would be okay, that he had some innocuous ritual planned, that he wouldn't have the heart to hurt me even in his present state of mind. I clung tightly to that belief even as I stared at Janie, all bloodied, and slumped over.

Todd took out his cell phone and called his family, waiting upstairs, and told them that they should turn on the television set now, everything was ready.

A glint of light reflected off the long blade as his hands flew above his head. Todd stood motionless, holding the knife high, eyes closed, chanting—almost inaudibly. Then he opened his eyes. He was ready. All softness had disappeared from his eyes, from his face. In its place, a firm resolve, to do what he felt he must do, appeared.

Todd stretched his arms higher.

"As I remove your heart and absorb it into me, you're heart will become my heart. United forever with mine and we will be together, always; one heart; one mind; one blood. Strong and sure—"

I vomited, my terror spurting violently against my sealed mouth and bouncing off and back down my throat, choking me, and distracting Todd. Helplessly gagging, the terror in my eyes turned into a desperate plea and I locked onto Todd's eyes and held them fast, afraid to let them go, pleading.

Horrified, Todd dropped his hands, the knife landing horizontally on my torso, as his hands shot out and ripped the tape from my mouth. Todd grabbed hold of my head and turned it to the side, as I continued to gag.

His parents, his aunt and uncle, and Jack Lester swarmed around, screaming at the situation, screaming at Todd. His uncle raced to undo one of my arm restraints, which prompted Todd to undo the other. Todd lifted me up and bent me over, hitting my back, but not really knowing what to do to help. Emily quickly removed my leg restraints.

And after much spitting and coughing, finally, the gagging stopped and even though I still could not catch my breath, I was at least now able to take a breath without choking.

Jack Lester started to dial a number on his cell phone, but before he was able to finish, Todd's father interrupted him, yelling, demanding to know whom he was calling.

Pausing, he forcefully replied, "I'm calling 911. This has to stop. He needs help, more help than you can give him. Can't you see that? Do you see where all the secrecy and fumbling around has led? It's got to stop!" But, as he began to dial again, Todd's father knocked the phone from his hands and they began arguing, and soon after the others joined in.

I was shaking and Todd, who looked like his head was going to explode, managed to reach beyond his shock, and went to put his arms around me. My survival instincts were still on high alert and my body reflexively recoiled from his touch, and as he continued moving towards me, without thinking, I was off the table, and in a flash, I was on the floor and curled up against the wall.

Todd stared at me. Not blinking. Completely calm now. On his face, no expression at all. My reaction, the sudden revulsion and rejection of him, and seeing him standing there like that, tore at my heart and I wanted take back my actions—rewind the tape.

The world was jangling, whirling, and jarring me—the noise in my head, the music still playing, and the raucous chorus of arguing voices—but I remained, silent, and frozen by the wall.

Then I saw it. And even as I saw it and even though I knew that it was real, it seemed unreal—not believable.

In a fleeting, irretrievable instant, Todd grabbed the knife and proceeded to plunge it into his own chest, collapsing on the floor moments later. Blood spurted. His family raced to him, crying, frantic, trying to stop the blood.

He lifted his head, looking at me, and in a moment of clarity, sought forgiveness. I looked into his eyes, and reaching my hand out towards him, tried to silently communicate my forgiveness and give his heart some peace. Then his head fell back onto the floor, his eyes staring, but not seeing. He was dead. My Todd was dead.

Epilogue

It has been over a year since Todd died and I've been thinking about him a lot lately, missing him. He was such a loving, wonderful person. I still find it hard to understand what happened, hard to believe it actually did happen. It feels kind of like a dream now. If only it really were a dream. It took me a long time to get over the shock of his death. I wish I could have done more to help.

Todd's family blamed me for his death, thinking that I must have said or done something that caused him to spiral out of control, and to this day, they still cannot forgive me. I hope in time they will.

Janie regained consciousness a few hours after Todd passed away, and thankfully, fully recovered from her head wounds. She attended Todd's funeral, but stayed along the periphery, not wanting to talk with anyone, not even me.

A couple of months ago, I met a wonderful guy named Richard. He's sweet, smart, and when we're together time just seems to fly by. I can feel my optimism slowly returning and am starting to look forward to the future again.

He doesn't like to talk about his past much, but he did tell me about a boating accident he had when he was young which left him with a terrible fear of the water. He was with two close friends of his and he was the only one who survived. It's so sad, but I know with a little bit of help and encouragement, he'll be able to enjoy being on the water again, something that he used to love so much.

Made in the USA
Coppell, TX
11 October 2020